"It's cust██████████**eal that wish with a kiss,"** she ████████████████ly pressed her mo████

Once his mouth touched hers and those soft, honeyed folds parted so easily, he couldn't help diving in. Her lips were quicksand, and he was drowning in them. He pulled her a little closer with the hand that was resting on her waist. He moved his free hand up and entangled it in her luxuriously thick, soft hair as he had longed to do since meeting her. He decided to let himself go a little deeper—for a little while longer.

When he slightly pushed her away, she weakly clung to his lapels, her eyes wide with wonder and longing. While the kiss was far too brief, at the same time it lasted much too long. He rationalized that he couldn't afford any emotional involvements, especially not now. Marcy Johnson could quickly become that—if he let her, which was something he must not do.

"Wow." Marcy sighed in breathless awe. "That was…" Her voice faded off as words escaped her.

"Deadly." Nathan finished for her, his eyes darkening with barely restrained hunger. Somehow, he resisted the urge to feast on her luscious lips again, knowing he would be lost if he did.

Books by Judy Lynn Hubbard

Harlequin Kimani Romance

These Arms of Mine
Our First Dance
Our First Kiss

JUDY LYNN HUBBARD

is a Texas native who has always been an avid reader—particularly of romance. Judy loves well-written, engaging stories with characters she can identify with, empathize with and root for. When writing, she honestly can't wait to see what happens next; she knows if she feels that way, she's created characters and a story that readers will thoroughly enjoy, and that's her ultimate goal.

OUR FIRST *Kiss*

JUDY LYNN HUBBARD

HARLEQUIN® KIMANI™ ROMANCE

To my brother, Randy, a man of few words,
but many kind deeds who always gives unselfishly of himself.
You've always been the best brother a sister could wish for
and I love you, always.

Recycling programs
for this product may
not exist in your area.

ISBN-13: 978-0-373-86319-8

OUR FIRST KISS

Copyright © 2013 by Judy Lynn Hubbard

For questions and comments about the quality of this book please contact us at CustomerService@Harlequin.com.

HARLEQUIN®
www.Harlequin.com

Printed in U.S.A.

Dear Reader,

I am pleased to present the sequel to *Our First Dance, Our First Kiss,* chronicling Marcy Johnson and Nathan Carter's love story. These two wouldn't leave me alone until I wrote their story—especially Marcy; she's very headstrong and tenacious, a fact the secretive Nathan quickly realizes. I love strong female characters like Marcy and the men who have their hands full trying to handle them. How about you?

I've had many requests for Nicole Carter's story and you know I can't disappoint you. I completed *Our First Kiss,* I started outlining Nicole and Alexander's book, which will take us into the world of high fashion in Paris, France.

I hope you enjoy reading *Our First Kiss* as much as I enjoyed writing it. Please let me know what you think.

Happy reading!

Judy Lynn Hubbard

www.JudyLynnHubbard.com

Twitter: @JudyLynnHubbard

Prologue

Marcy glanced at her watch for at least the tenth time in the past half hour. Her mother and father glanced at each other and then back to their twenty-eight-year-old daughter, who was determinedly searching the room with her eyes.

"Do you have to be somewhere, dear?" Margaret made reference to her daughter's obvious preoccupation.

"Definitely." She secretively smiled.

"Where?" Michael laughed at the tenacious gleam in her eyes.

"I have to go and find Nathan."

Her watch informed her it was a few minutes before midnight. She intended to be in Nathan's arms when the clock struck twelve.

"What for?" Margaret eyed her daughter suspiciously. She hadn't seen her this worked up over a man since... well, since never.

"For the usual midnight occurrence on New Year's Eve." Marcy's eyes twinkled.

"Marcy, you've just met him," Margaret gasped.

"Mom, tell me again how you and Dad met and how long it took you two to get involved?" Marcy laughingly reminded.

"She has you there, Margaret." Michael kissed his wife's cheek.

"You two are incorrigible." Margaret laughed, a little embarrassed.

"We just know what we want and go after it, right, Dad?" Marcy winked at her father.

"Right, kitten," he agreed. "Go and find Nathan, and give him my regards."

"Oh, I will—right after I give him mine," Marcy promised before hurrying off.

One minute before midnight, Marcy strategically positioned herself next to Nathan. She reached him just as the group countdown reached zero and white-and-black balloons along with colorful streamers miraculously began raining down on them.

"Happy New Year, Nathan." She could tell her voice startled him as he turned around to face her.

"Happy New Year, Marcy," he echoed.

Lord, she was gorgeous. Why did she have to be so darn beautiful, and why did he have to meet her now? More importantly, why did he have to be so attracted to her when he knew there was no way he could act on that attraction?

Instinctively, Marcy knew he was about to shake her hand. She negatively shook her head and placed possessive hands on his broad shoulders. He raised an eyebrow at her forwardness, and she smiled confidently.

"It's customary to seal that wish with a kiss," she said, as she immediately pressed her mouth to his.

Once his mouth touched hers and those soft honey folds parted so easily, he couldn't help but dive in. Her lips were quicksand, and he was drowning in them. He pulled her a little closer with the hand that was resting on her waist. He moved his free hand up and entangled it in her luxuriously thick, soft hair as he had wanted to do since meeting her. He decided to let himself go a little deeper—for a little while more.

When minutes later he pushed her away, she weakly clinging to his lapels, her eyes wide with wonder and longing. While the kiss was far too brief, at the same time it lasted much too long. He rationalized that he couldn't afford any emotional involvements—especially now. Marcy Johnson could quickly become that—if he let her—which was something he must not do.

"Wow." Marcy sighed in breathless awe. "That was…" Her voice faded off as words escaped her.

"Deadly." Nathan's finished for her, his eyes darkening with barely restrained hunger. Somehow, he resisted the urge to feast on her luscious lips again, knowing he would be lost if he did. Unfortunately, he was halfway there already.

Chapter 1

Marcy Johnson was a determined woman on a single-minded mission. Her high-heeled navy pumps clicked furiously on the pavement as she resolutely made her way through the crowded Manhattan streets.

Her mind was focused on one thing—or more precisely on one person: Nathan Carter. She had only met him a week ago, but that first glance had been enough. He was definitely a man she wanted to get to know better. Now, she had one goal—getting the elusive hunk to admit he was interested in her, too.

They had shared a searing kiss on New Year's Eve, but since then, he had avoided her like the plague; however, she had never been one to be put off for long, especially not when there was something she wanted. A smile tilted the corners of her mouth; Nathan Carter was about to find that out firsthand.

Not that she needed an excuse, but she did have a built-in reason to seek him out; his sister and her brother were getting married in three days, and as they were both in the wedding party, they naturally had things to discuss and do pertaining to the bride and groom.

Knowing which suite Nathan occupied, Marcy breezed into the very expensive ornate Muse hotel and made her way to the elevators without stopping at the reception desk. She had no intention of having herself announced so he could make up a convenient excuse not to see her. She smiled and punched the button that would take her to the designated floor. When the doors closed, she took a compact from her navy bag, freshened up her red lipstick and made sure her hair was in place before exiting the elevator when it stopped.

While she walked to Nathan's door, she removed her black leather coat and peeled matching gloves from fingers. Brushing an imaginary piece of lint from the lapel of the figure-hugging navy skirt suit, she took a deep breath, released it and resolutely knocked on the door, waiting impatiently for Nathan to answer. When he did, she fought back a laugh when shock followed by vague annoyance registered on his handsome face.

"Good morning, Nathan," she brightly greeted, walking past him into the room without waiting for an invitation.

"Come on in," he said as he sarcastically waved his hand, closing the door behind her.

He scratched his hair-covered chin. Lord, help him! What was Marcy Johnson doing here, and more importantly why was he so glad to see her? *Because you're attracted to her, you idiot!*

As always, she looked fabulous and smelled sinfully wonderful. Every nerve ending in his traitorous body stood at rapt attention as they did whenever they were in the same room together. He silently cursed her disastrous effect on his usual steadfast equilibrium.

"What's wrong, handsome? Get up on the wrong side of the bed?"

Appreciative eyes slowly traveled over the white terry cloth robe he wore, lingering at the V opening that parted revealing a tantalizing glimpse of his smooth, muscled dark brown chest. She fought down an insane urge to jump inside the robe with him and let nature take its course— mmm, mmm, mmm!

"What are you doing here, Marcy?" He pulled his robe together and belted it tighter, eliciting a teasing smile from his gorgeous intruder.

"Well, since our respective siblings are getting married in a few days, I thought you might want to go shopping for a wedding present with me."

He swallowed a groan as she sat on the edge of his unmade bed and crossed those shapely long legs, hitching the already outrageously short skirt higher on her upper thighs. Her actions caused a quickening of his pulse and an uncomfortable tightening in his groin.

Say no, he silently ordered. *In a matter of weeks, maybe days, you're on your way to Yemen with the rest of your team on a secret mission to rescue the U.S. envoy and his aides from insurgents. You don't have the time or the right to start anything you know you can't finish with Marcy, so nip it in the bud—now! Remember your training, and exhibit the self-control you know you possess. Even though you want to say yes, say no.*

"I plan on doing my shopping later," he replied.

"When?" At his silence, she smiled cajolingly. "Come on, Nathan. You have to buy them a present and so do I. Why not come along with me now?"

She stood, walked over to him and touched his arm,

feeling firm muscles contract beneath her fingers. Lord, he was rock-solid hard. How did a lawyer get an athletic body like his? Everything about him was just yummy from his close-cropped black hair to his neatly trimmed goatee that just begged for her fingers' touch. Her heart skipped several beats as she once again marveled at his dizzying effect on her.

"Don't you have to be somewhere—like at work?"

"Not this morning." Unable to resist, she took a step closer. "I'm going in later. I cleared my schedule especially for you. You're not going to let me go to all that trouble for nothing, are you?"

"I appreciate…" He paused, groaning inwardly. He was so close to caving that it was embarrassing.

"Good, then let's go." Her fingers tightened on his arm.

A smile played about his lips. "Do you mind if I change first?"

"Don't do it on my account." Her eyes slowly traveled over his magnificent form, lingering on the revealed flesh of his legs and chest before locking with his eyes again.

"Well, I hardly think I can go out like this." He shook his head at her.

She smiled and moved slightly closer to him until their bodies were almost touching. He smelled fresh and clean from a recent shower. His eyes darkened at her actions and seemed slightly unsteady. *Good, I do affect him.*

Removing her fingers from his arm, he moved purposefully away from temptation by walking a few feet away, bending down to pick up the clothes that were neatly laid out on the bed. He turned toward the bathroom.

"I'll be ready in a minute," he shot over his shoulder.

"I'll be waiting," she promised and laughed when he sighed loudly before closing the bathroom door behind him. She walked over to the closed door and leaned against it, "I can't believe your parents let you stay in a hotel—albeit a luxurious one."

"They weren't happy about it, but I finally convinced them it was for the best." His voice was muffled by the closed door.

"Why?"

She placed her hand on the brass knob, toying with the scandalous idea of opening it. What would he do if she sauntered in while he was dressing? The thought of the possible wonderful repercussions of such action on her part almost made her test him. But she decided to be good—for now.

"I'm officially on vacation, but there are some…things that I still need to be on top of. I'll be getting phone calls at all hours, and it's just easier if I have my own place." Inside the bathroom, he smiled as he remembered his mother's indignation as he had tried to explain that fact to her. She had not been pleased to say the least.

"A workaholic," Marcy sympathized, reluctantly dropping her hand from the doorknob and walking a few steps away.

He chuckled. "You, too?"

"Uh-huh."

She peered into his partially open closet. His clothes were neatly hung and ordered by type—shirts, dress pants, jeans, sweaters and several immaculate suits. His shoes were neatly lined at the bottom—also sorted by types. She smiled and made her way over to his dresser and picked up various objects, studying them. Again, everything was neatly lined up in its proper place indicative of a man who thrived on order; she could relate, but she was determined to inject a little well-aimed chaos into his orderly life while he was in town.

"Are you always so disciplined and in control, Nathan?"

"Always." His response was quick and sure.

She chuckled. "I knew you were going to say that."

Unable to resist, she opened a drawer and found his socks neatly folded and equally spaced. Another drawer housed his underwear—black boxers, each pair purposefully folded in the same dimensions. She ran her fingers lightly over the soft material, and her smile widened. He gave a new meaning to the word *organized*.

"What are you doing out there?"

"Waiting for you," she innocently responded, closing one drawer and then the other. "Were you ever in the military?"

He was silent for a full twenty seconds before warily asking, "Why do you ask?"

"Because your room is extremely well ordered with everything in its proper place. You're more organized than I am, and that's saying something," she said and laughed. "Nathan?" she prompted when he remained noticeably silent.

"I did a short stint in the marines after high school," he finally answered.

That was an interesting tidbit. She stared at the still-closed bathroom door, curiosity piqued.

"Did you ever consider going career military."

"No, military life wasn't for me. I wanted to be a lawyer. I enjoy sparring with words more than with weapons or my fists."

Okay, that was a necessary little white lie. He loved hand-to-hand combat, the nonstop action and the insane danger his secret military career exposed him to—or at least he had loved it; however, recently nagging doubts about his inability to carve out a normal personal life due to his unusual profession had started surfacing, making him question his priorities.

When he reentered the bedroom, Marcy lowered a bottle of cologne from her nose and returned it to its proper place. He arched an eyebrow at her intrusiveness.

"I'm ready." He was dressed in a cream sweater and chocolate pants. He slipped his muscled arms into the sleeves of a brown leather bomber jacket.

God, he looked good! It should be a crime for a man to be so gorgeous. He held up her coat, and she walked over and slipped it on. Unable to help herself, she then looped her hand through his arm as they walked to the door.

He inwardly groaned at the feel of her body against his. Shoving his hands into his jacket pocket, he fought down an overwhelming urge to grab and bury all ten of his fingers deeply into that gorgeous hair of hers and pull her soft, tempting mouth against his.

"You're going to have a good time, Nathan," she promised as they entered the elevator.

Not if I can help it, he silently promised.

As if she could read his mind, Marcy's smile widened— the sight was like a kick in the gut. Lord, she was a beautiful woman—one he had no business agreeing to go shopping with. He was just being polite to his future sister-in-law—no harm in that. Hell, if he could routinely deal with terrorists, assassins and threats against the United States or its citizens, he could handle going shopping with Marcy Johnson for a few hours. However, could he squelch his exponentially growing attraction to her? That was the real question for which he didn't have a satisfactory answer.

"Isn't this lovely, Nathan?" Marcy held up a silver photo album.

"Yes, lovely, just like the candlesticks were, and the picture frame and the tray at the other store," he reminded her.

He was annoyed. What he had prayed would be a short trip had turned into a marathon. Why couldn't women ever make up their minds? They had been window-shopping over two hours—he had spent two long agonizing hours fighting his attraction to this captivating, spirited woman, and each passing second in her presence felt like torture.

"True, but this is really nice, isn't it?" She lightly fingered the inlaid rose pattern, undaunted by his exasperated tones.

"Yes, Marcy, it's lovely," he dryly repeated. "I don't know why you're wasting so much time over it. You're not going to buy it."

"Women like to browse and find the best bargains." She wrinkled her nose at him as she replaced the album on the shelf. "What is it about men that you hate shopping?"

"We don't mind shopping. What we do mind is the uncertainty you women exhibit at every turn. Men know what we're looking for, go out, find it and buy it."

"Well, you must not know what you're looking for because you haven't bought anything yet, either," she sweetly reminded him.

"Maybe I'm not going to give them silver or crystal," he quickly replied.

"No?" She placed her hands on her shapely hips. "Then what do you have in mind?"

"I was thinking more along the lines of…" His voice trailed off, and he thought fast but not fast enough.

"You have no idea what you're going to get, do you?"

"Of course I do."

"Really, then tell me what it is," she challenged.

"I was thinking of something else, but since you dragged me to all of these crystal stores, I've decided on wineglasses."

She smiled and pointed behind him. "They have some lovely ones here."

"I saw them. They're not what I'm looking for."

"What type were you thinking about? Goblets? Champagne glasses? Flutes? Are you looking for a particular brand of crystal? Waterford? Baccarat? Mikasa? Bavari? Lennox?" She expertly rattled off possible choices.

"Stop hurling possibilities at me." He smiled despite himself. "I'll know them when I see them."

"Sure you will." She chuckled and couldn't resist impishly adding, "There's nothing indecisive about you."

"Are you going to get that?" He pointed to the music box in her hands.

"No." Marcy set the box down, linked her hand through his arm and pulled him away, smiling at his knowing smirk. "Let's try this other little shop down the way."

They exited one of the wonderful specialty shops in Greenwich Village and walked toward another. Marcy could get lost in this part of Manhattan for days. As they walked down the pedestrian-filled sidewalks surrounded by various shades of redbrick buildings on either side of the busy one-way street filled with cars, buses and cabs, Marcy glanced at the barren trees that littered the sidewalk; she couldn't wait for them to bloom with the arrival of spring.

She had purposefully taken him to five different places simply to prolong their time together. Now she guided him into the store where the wedding present she had ordered for Damien and Natasha was being held.

"Ms. Johnson." The female clerk beamed as they entered. "I know why you're here. Let me go and get it." She disappeared into another room.

Nathan's lips thinned. "You've already bought Natasha and Damien's present?"

"Yes." Marcy laughed at his exasperation. "Wait until you see it."

He sighed loudly and then asked, "Then why did you drag me to all those other shops?"

"I thought you might like some ideas," she innocently responded. At his look of displeasure, she asked, "Is my company so unbearable?"

Quite the contrary; he enjoyed being with her. She was a breath of fresh air, and in her presence, he felt as carefree as sails of a boat being hoisted by liberating winds. He shouldn't be here with her, but honestly, he had no desire to be anywhere else.

"I don't like being played." He tried to sound stern but failed miserably.

"And I love to play," she admitted around a chuckle, touching his arm and moving closer to him. "What are we going to do about that blatant contradiction?"

He shook his head at her as a smile played about his lips. He had never met a more brazen or fascinating woman.

"I'm sure you'll think of something," he drawled.

"Oh, I'm sure I will," she agreed.

"Here you are, Ms. Johnson." The clerk returned carefully cradling a twelve-inch crystal sculpture of a male and female ballerina, limbs frozen in movement dancing close to each other.

"Oh, it's gorgeous." Marcy approved, gently taking the figure from the woman's hands and lifting it for Nathan's inspection. "Isn't it, Nathan?"

"Yes, it's very nice." He smiled at the joy lighting up her face—joy at doing something for someone she loved.

She carefully placed it down on the glass countertop and flipped a switch in the back to send soft music filtering into the air. She cocked her ear listening and then enthused, "It's perfect!"

"Is that music from the ballet?"

"Yes, it's the theme song," she informed him before returning her attention to the clerk. "You've done a wonderful job in such a short time."

"We're pleased you're happy, Ms. Johnson," the woman assured her as she took Marcy's credit card. "Shall we gift wrap it for you?"

"Oh, yes in something white and silver. It's a wedding gift."

"We have just the thing," the woman said. "Would you like to wait for it?"

Marcy glanced at Nathan and returned her attention to the clerk. "Yes, we'll wait."

"I don't know how I'm going to top that."

"Do you really think they'll like it?" She turned anxious eyes on him.

"They'll love it," he responded positively, taking her hand in his reassuringly.

She glanced at their linked fingers and then back into his now slightly uncomfortable eyes. When he tried to drop her hand, she tightened her fingers in his.

"I like Natasha. She's a wonderful woman."

"Thanks. Damien seems devoted to her."

"He is, and she's perfect for him."

"They certainly didn't waste any time deciding to marry, did they?"

She frowned. "Why should they?"

"No reason." At her curious stare, he elaborated, "It's just not like Natasha to be so brash. I mean she and Damien haven't known each other long."

"It doesn't matter how long you know someone. When your heart tells you that you've found your soul mate, you have to listen to it." Her eyes never left his as she delivered her double entendre that wasn't lost on him. "Besides, we Johnsons are a decisive lot, and when we make up our minds, we go full steam ahead until we achieve our goal."

"Yes." He warily stared into her twinkling eyes. "I'm realizing that."

"That's good," she softly approved.

Her sexy voice stroked him in all the deliciously wrong places. Why did he have to meet her now when he logically knew he couldn't do anything about the obvious attraction they both felt? Why did she insist on making things harder by refusing to stay away from him as he had been trying so hard to stay away from her?

"I'm going to look at some wineglasses." Needing some distance, he disentangled his hand from hers and walked away; of course, she followed him.

"Those are lovely,"

She leaned close to him, brushing her arm against his. The maddening scent of her perfume assailed his over-heightened senses. He wanted to grab her and kiss her desperately. He wanted to press her soft, yielding body close to his and plunder. He wanted… *Damn! Get a hold of yourself, man!*

"I think I like those better." He pointed at a pair of champagne flutes a few feet away from her—to gain some space between them.

To his amazement, she stayed put, but when he glanced back at her, she was smiling amusedly as if she was completely aware of what his intentions had been.

"How about an early lunch?" Marcy suggested as they left the store a short while later, Nathan carrying her package and a set of Baccarat champagne flutes he had bought.

"I really have a lot to do today," he replied.

That was a lie. The truth was he was enjoying himself with her much too much. He needed to get away from her bubbly, contagious, easy-to-be-with personality. If things were different, though…

"You have to eat, don't you?" She interrupted his thoughts.

"I'll just grab something later at the hotel."

"Hotel food!" She screwed up her face in disgust. "Have you ever been there?" She pointed to the first restaurant she saw.

"No, but some other time," he declined, preparing to hand her package to her and leave her on Hudson Street.

"There's no time like the present." Disregarding the shopping bag containing her gift, she took his free hand and guided him into the restaurant doors.

"Marcy, really…" His protest died on his lips as the hostess walked over to them.

"How many?" the woman asked.

"Two, please." Marcy refused to release his hand until they were seated at a charming white linen-covered table for two with a view of downtown Manhattan. "Isn't this lovely?"

He frowned at her. "Do you ever take no for an answer?"

"Not if I can help it," she said as she treated him to a brilliant smile.

"What can I get you two to drink?" a white-coated waiter asked.

"Would you like to order the drinks, too?" Nathan grouchily asked.

"If you'd like me to," she shot back, smiling at his obvious bad humor.

"I'll have a Perrier with a twist," he snapped without asking what she wanted.

"And you, ma'am?" The waiter turned to her after raising an eyebrow at Nathan's rudeness.

"The same," she said and smiled. Once the waiter disappeared, she picked up her menu. "Nathan, are you going to scowl all the way through lunch?"

"I don't appreciate being forced into this." He pointedly glanced at his menu.

"Forced?" A perfectly arched eyebrow rose. "Look at the two of us. I'm not even half your size." She lowered her menu to the table and met his hooded eyes. "If you really wanted to decline, you could have easily done so."

Of course he could have declined, but he hadn't wanted to; therein lay his problem.

"Maybe I didn't want to hurt your feelings," he countered.

"How sweet." She suddenly smiled.

"I am not sweet," he quickly denied.

"We'll see," she softly promised. At his silence, she continued, "Nathan, it's just an innocent lunch."

"Nothing is innocent with you, Marcy Johnson," he surmised and then suddenly smiled.

"Just plain Marcy," she corrected. "You have a gorgeous smile." She rested her chin on her clasped hands. "Why do you frown so much?"

"I don't frown," he disagreed. "I just don't walk around grinning like an idiot all day long."

She gazed into his deep chocolate eyes and was immediately lost. Lord, this man just frazzled her until she didn't know her own name.

"No one could ever accuse you of being an idiot," she charmed, sitting back in her chair. "Tell me about yourself."

"There's not much to tell," he quickly countered, taking a grateful sip of the drink that was placed in front of him.

"Are you two ready to order?" their waiter asked.

"What are you going to have?" Nathan decided to be a gentleman this time.

"You order for me," she suggested.

"I don't know what you'd like."

"Oh, I think you can figure out what I'd like," she naughtily countered, eliciting a nervous cough from their waiter and slight chuckle from her date.

She was a breath of fresh air, and he absurdly wanted her like he had wanted no other woman. He'd love to see her by candlelight dressed to kill, smiling only for him as he took her into his arms to dance. *Whoa, take it easy, man. You won't be alone with her again, especially not for a romantic dinner—got it?*

"The waiter's waiting, Nathan," Marcy interrupted his thoughts.

"Yes." He cleared his throat. "I'll have the shrimp platter, and the lady will have the coq au vin."

"I've always wanted to try that," Marcy said, approving his choice.

"I like it. I hope you enjoy it."

"I'm sure I will. If I don't, you'll share your shrimp with me, won't you?"

"Don't count on it." He shook his head.

"I'm sure I could persuade you." She leaned forward and trailed a finger lightly across the back of his hand before picking up her glass and taking a sip of water.

"It might be fun to let you try," he admitted, smiling slightly.

"That's the spirit," she approved, glad he was loosening up. "You were going to tell me about yourself," she reminded.

"Like I said, there's not much to tell," he reiterated, barely disguising a sigh at her tenacity.

"I doubt that," she said as she lowered her drink to the table. "Lawyer for the State Department—you must have a dozen interesting tales."

She didn't know the half of it. What would she say if she knew he had spent the past ten years of his life as a member of an officially nonexistent military unit that not even his family knew about? He could relate stories of danger and intrigue that would rival the plot of any movie—if he could talk about his Black Ops job that is, which he couldn't.

"My job's confidential."

She noted his fingers tightened around his glass. Doesn't like to talk about his work, she mentally noted—strange and intriguing.

"Are you enjoying being home?" she asked, changing subjects, and his fingers noticeably relaxed.

"Yes," he said and nodded. "It's great to be back."

She absently slid fingers through her silky hair, and he hid a groan, longing to do the same thing; he knew from experience how incredibly soft it was. His mind wandered to the one time he had touched her hair, had held her in his arms and tasted her incredibly sweet lips—a week ago on New Year's Eve.

Staring at the vibrant woman sitting across from him only intensified the seeds of dissatisfaction with his life. His job was necessary, and he knew he made a difference, but he was growing tired of the necessary secrecy, weary of running around from one side of the world to the other—most of the time with little or no notice. He was fed up with having nowhere to really call home and more importantly of having no one to share his life with.

His country had always come first before everything. He didn't regret his years of service, but perhaps it was time for some serious reevaluation. Maybe he was just getting old; after all, he was thirty-one, and his priorities had naturally changed. A dissatisfied soldier was a dangerous one, and there was no denying the fact that he had become increasingly dissatisfied of late and meeting Marcy had really emphasized that fact for him.

"Nathan?" Marcy touched his hand and called his name more forcefully, "Nathan!"

"Hmm?" He snapped out of his disturbing introspection.

"Where were you?" She pretended to pout. "Am I so boring that I can't hold your attention?"

"Marcy, no one would ever call you boring." He laughed and she joined him. "I was just thinking."

"About?"

"Nothing important," he assured. "What were you saying before I spaced out?"

"I was asking if you've missed New York." Her well-manicured fingernails played with the ends of a napkin.

"Very much," he admitted, wanting to cover those long, feminine fingers with his, pull her into his lap and…

"Are you involved with a woman?" she asked out of the blue.

"That's rather personal, isn't it?" He fought back a grin, realizing he had smiled more today than he had in the four years he had been away from home, and the reason was sitting across the table from him.

"Not as personal as I plan to get," she promised, and he could do nothing except chuckle. "Well, are you?"

"No, my job takes up all of my time."

His words were music to her ears. He was free, and she was determined that when all was said and done he would be hers.

"It's just a job, Nathan," she whispered.

"A career," he corrected. An increasingly burdensome career.

"Even a career we love can become all-consuming if we let it." She spoke from experience.

"Maybe I don't have a problem with that." He glanced around hoping to see their food coming so he could escape her probing questions.

"Maybe you should. Life's too short to let it pass you by. Haven't you ever wanted to find a nice woman, settle down and have some kids?" He remained noticeably silent, staring intently at the contents of his glass, prompting her to change the subject again. "Do you like basketball?"

"What?" He glanced up from his drink, baffled at sudden shift in direction.

"Basketball. Do you like it?" she repeated, smiling.

"You do that very well," he said, intending to flatter, without answering her question.

"Tools of the trade." She smiled.

"Stockbroker, right?" He was more comfortable talking about her.

"Correct."

"Do you like it?"

"I love it," she enthused. "My day's always different, always interesting—never a dull moment."

"You thrive on change," he stated, not asking. That was very apparent to anyone having the pleasure to meet her.

"And challenges," she said and glanced at him pointedly. "I prefer more continuity in my personal life, though."

His heart sank a little at her easy admission. That was one thing he could never give her. Absurdly, he wished he could.

"Most people do," he shortly agreed.

"Do you?" She tilted her head, and her thick mane of hair fell to one side.

"As I said before, I don't have much of a personal life," he truthfully responded. "Work takes up most of my time."

"That leads to a lonely existence, Nathan."

"I suppose." He sighed, eyes growing distant. He knew

how true her words were—how true he feared they would always be for him.

"Are you?" She watched him closely.

"Am I what?" He refocused on her.

"Lonely?" She reached across and covered his hand with hers, which relaxed for a few seconds before he pulled away.

"I'm content." He realized he was trying to convince himself rather than her.

"Evasive," she murmured.

"You're tenacious," he countered, and she smiled.

"I told you I was," she said and shrugged. "I won't let you be lonely while you're here, Nathan," she softly promised.

"I'm sure you won't," he agreed with a smirk. "Marcy Johnson, I don't quite know what to make of you." He paused before grudgingly admitting as their food was placed before them. "You are something else."

"Mmm-hmm." She acknowledged the validity of his words. "You know what else I am?" She picked up her napkin and placed it on her lap.

"What?" He ventured to ask.

"I'm all yours. All you have to do is admit that you want me, reach out your hand and take me," she bluntly responded when they were alone before picking up her fork and cutting into her buttery soft chicken.

His mouth dropped open in shock as he digested her stunning words, and he was unable to stop it. She had completely floored him with her unabashed forwardness and determination. She also excited, enthralled and enchanted him.

"You shouldn't say things like that, Marcy."

"Why not?"

"Because people will take advantage of you if you let them."

"Is that what you plan to do?"

"No."

She sighed regretfully. "That's a shame."

"Marcy Johnson, you are—" he paused before admitting "—unlike any woman I've ever met."

"Is that good or bad?"

"Definitely good," he said and smiled. "There's nothing fake about you."

"What you see is what you get, Nathan."

What he saw, he wanted—badly. Dammit, why did he have to return home and run headlong into this fascinating, exciting woman who appeared to want nothing more than the chance to make him happy, and why did he want nothing more than the time to let her try?

"It's fate," she whispered, laughing softly at his shocked expression when she answered his silent question.

Chapter 2

Though he tried to prepare himself for his next meeting with Marcy, she still knocked every ounce of breath out of his lungs when their eyes locked at the rehearsal dinner for Natasha and Damien later that evening. She was dressed in a black knee-length leather skirt with a wicked slit up the back, matching tight-fitting jacket and high-heeled black leather pumps. All of that raven hair was piled high on top of her head in an intentionally careless bun, allowing tendrils to escape to caress her face and nape. She looked lovely and desirable.

"Hi, handsome," her sultry voice greeted him as he entered the small ballroom of the restaurant.

"Marcy." He nodded at her politely as he unsuccessfully tried to still the rapid beating of his heart.

"Did you miss me?" He looked wonderful in his black suit, white shirt and black-and-gray tie.

"It's only been a few hours since I last saw you?" Time

he had spent trying to unsuccessfully stop thinking about her—the look of her, the feel of her fingers on his, the exotic smell of her.

"I know." She leaned close and whispered confidentially in his ear, "I missed you terribly."

His knees almost buckled at her words and as the provocative scent she wore wafted up his nostrils and her soft body brushed lightly yet maddeningly against his. He fought with every ounce of strength he possessed to keep from crushing that curvaceous body to his and fastening his mouth to her luscious lips—lips he knew from experience were soft, decadent and addictive.

Unable to help himself, he groaned. "What is that perfume you're wearing?"

She leaned slightly back to stare into his intense eyes. "Chanel." She smiled and leaned in closer again. "Do you like it?"

"It's…nice."

"I'm glad you approve." She deliberately ran her fingers across her exposed collarbone drawing his burning gaze there.

Who did he think he was fooling? Judging by his darkening eyes, watching the slow progression of her finger across her skin, he thought it was much more than nice. She secretly vowed to buy up every bottle she could get her hands on in the morning.

"Marcy, darling, bring Nathan over here," her mother ordered.

"Coming, Mom." She smiled up at him. "I'm afraid it's time to mingle."

She thankfully moved back from him but grabbed his hand, shooting tiny thrills of pleasure up his arm. This woman was deadlier than any adversary he had ever faced in the field of combat—and that was saying something.

"That's what we're here for." He was proud his voice sounded steady.

"But there is later…" She let her sentence trail off suggestively.

They walked over to stand beside his sister Nicole, who was talking to the guests of honor, Damien and Natasha. Nathan's parents, Linda and Lincoln, were conversing with Marcy's mother and father, Margaret and Michael, a short distance away. Marcy's smile widened as she glanced at their matchmaking mothers who seemed particularly interested in watching the interplay between her and Nathan; it appeared they were their next project.

"I'm starving. What's for dinner, Mama?" Natasha asked.

"Seafood, all different kinds." Linda smiled at her daughter.

"Mmm, I can't wait," Natasha said as her eyes sparkled expectantly.

"This one has really been developing an appetite lately." Damien wrapped his arms around his fiancée's waist from behind.

"Love makes me hungry." She smiled as he kissed her neck lingeringly.

"When Nathan and I were shopping today, we had some wonderful seafood at lunch—well, he did. I managed to steal a bite or two off of his plate." Marcy's statement caused all eyes to focus on her and Nathan.

"You and Nathan went shopping?" Nicole's mouth dropped open as did her sister's and mother's.

"Yes, for Natasha and Dami's wedding present," Marcy confirmed.

"And she dragged me from store to store when she already had their present picked out at the last store we went to," Nathan good-naturedly interjected.

"Don't you just hate shopping with women?" Damien sympathized, kissing Natasha on the cheek to soften his words.

"Oh, you!" Natasha tapped his chest lightly in admonishment.

"They never know what they want," Lincoln agreed as the men levitated toward each other.

"And they drag you around from store to store for hours and hours and then *finally* decide on something they saw at the first store you were in," Michael chimed in.

"I don't know why we don't leave you at home. You're always fretting about how much money we spend." Linda added her thoughts as the women, except for Natasha and Marcy, congregated together glaring at their respective man.

"Aren't they just?" Margaret agreed, smiling tolerantly at her husband, Michael. "But if the present is for them, no amount of time is too great and the sky is the limit on how much we spend."

"Amen," Nicole agreed, and Natasha shook her head.

"Boy, did I open a can of worms," Marcy whispered to Nathan, whom she noted still stood by her side.

"Are you kidding?" Nathan chuckled. "They're having a blast."

Marcy glanced at everyone as they engaged in heated, though pleasant, banter about the subject and laughed in agreement. They were thankfully saved from further escalation of the tiny gender war brewing when dinner was wheeled in. As everyone took their seats at the rectangular table, Marcy was dismayed to find herself sitting by her brother a table's length away from Nathan. Who had made these ridiculous seating arrangements?

Nicole, who was sitting by her brother, glanced at Marcy's sunken expression and sprang into action, "Look at us—

Johnsons at one end and Carters at the other. We need to break this up."

"You're right, Nicole," Marcy agreed, trying not to burst into a radiant smile.

"Marcy, you take my seat by Nathan, and I'll take yours by Damien."

Marcy quickly stood and gave Nicole a wink as they passed each other. Nicole mouthed, "Don't mention it."

Once she was seated, Nicole continued to rearrange people. "Momma, you should sit by Mr. Johnson down here. Mrs. Johnson, why don't you go up and sit by Dad."

Nicole received tolerant smiles as people followed her directions. Her mother's eyes held understanding and approval at her youngest daughter's actions. Nicole continued to survey the table with a slight determined frown.

"Now, that's better. Isn't it?" Nicole asked and was pleased when everyone agreed—except a frowning Nathan she noted with a smile.

"I am glad you didn't move me to the opposite end away from my fiancé." Natasha laughed at her sister.

"Please, I would need an army to do that," Nicole said and chuckled.

"You're so right." Damien pulled Natasha closer and kissed her lips.

"Save some of that for the honeymoon," Michael suggested with a laugh.

"Oh, I think we'll manage just fine." Damien had Natasha's cheeks reddening,

"Damien!" Natasha scolded and he laughingly kissed her again.

"She doesn't know what to do with me," he informed everyone when he lifted his head.

"We Johnsons can be incorrigible," Marcy replied, staring at Nathan, who refused to glance her way.

"A trait you both inherited from your father," Margaret assured, and the occupants of the room dissolved in laughter again.

"Are you planning on ignoring me all night, Nathan?" As the happy banter around the table continued, Marcy turned amused eyes to his annoyed ones.

"I was debating it," he tightly replied.

"I had nothing to do with rearranging everyone. That was your sister's idea," she reminded.

"Mmm-hmm." His tone stated he didn't believe she was as innocent as she professed to be. He glanced down the table, meeting his sister's dancing eyes. He had plans to pay her back later. Not that he really minded sitting next to Marcy, but he was trying to do the right thing and stay away from her—for her sake and his.

"Look at it this way. You can use this time to sample some more of my perfume," she offered, moving closer.

He inwardly groaned. That was the last thing he needed. He studied her beautiful face, and his dark mood intensified as she obviously fought to hide a smile.

"Yippee." He nearly growled the word.

"A toast to Natasha and Damien." Michael stood with a glass raised. "Two pieces of the puzzle of love who fit perfectly together. May they share a long happy life filled with love and hopefully soon the pitter-patter of little feet."

"Cheers." Everyone agreed and raised their glasses.

"We'll see what we can do about your first grandchild, Dad," Damien promised as he and Natasha unlinked their wrists and lowered their glasses—eyes twinkling because of their shared secret about Natasha's condition.

"Wouldn't it be nice if we all gathered together soon to celebrate another union of our children?" Margaret candidly suggested.

"That would be lovely, Margaret." Linda followed the direction of her eyes.

"You never know what could happen." Marcy chuckled as she glanced at Nathan's slightly uncomfortable, tense features before smiling brilliantly at their mothers.

"I'll start designing your wedding dress," Nicole teased.

"And Linda and I can begin on the guest list and the menu," Margaret excitedly began.

"Hey, wait a minute!" Nathan indignantly interrupted, and everyone laughed heartily—everyone except Damien.

Marcy met her brother's narrowed eyes and gave him a wink. He was going to have trouble sharing her, but she would help him through the rough spots. He and Nathan would hit it off; she was determined about that.

"Linda, I'll call you tomorrow," Margaret promised.

"Please do." Linda smiled down the table at her.

Lincoln and Michael shook their heads at each other across the table as their wives made the union of Marcy and Nathan their new project. They picked up their glasses in a silent, resigned toast to their respective spouses.

"What do you think they are talking about so intensely?" Nicole asked as she stood with Marcy and Natasha watching Nathan and Damien from across the room.

"Me, of course." Marcy smiled. "Dami is playing big brother, reading Nathan the riot act."

"I'll go over and put a stop to this," Natasha promised, but Marcy touched her arm halting her.

"It's okay, Natasha. Let Dami assert himself. He will, anyway." She chuckled in resignation. "Better now when I can keep an eye on him. Besides, it is rather sweet, don't you think?" She stared lovingly at her brother's intense face.

"I do," Nicole agreed. "Poor Nathan. He doesn't know

what to do about any of this," she sympathized, eyes settling on her brother as he took a gulp of his drink.

"He'll figure it out. I guarantee that," Marcy confidently replied.

Natasha frowned as she glanced across at her brother. He didn't seem upset as he listened to Damien. That was good. Damien glanced at her, and she shook her head at him in exasperation. He blew her a kiss before returning his attention to Nathan.

"I do wish Dami would stop monopolizing Nathan's time." Marcy sighed. "I need to make my next move."

"Poor Nathan. He doesn't have a chance." Nicole shook her head at the determination etched on her friend's face.

"He doesn't need one," Marcy quickly responded, and they all chuckled as they glanced across the room at their respective brothers.

"Marcy can be a handful," Damien informed Nathan.

"No? Really?" Damien and Nathan laughed.

"I see you've already found that out."

"I have. She's very determined."

"She's also very honest—too honest for her own good sometimes," Damien continued, glancing across at his sister as she stood with Natasha and Nicole.

"Yes, she is," Nathan agreed. "She's very beautiful," Nathan couldn't help admitting as he, too, glanced across the room at the subject of their conversation.

"You're attracted to her." Damien returned cool eyes to his fiancée's brother.

"Who wouldn't be?" Nathan proclaimed quickly. Then he added, "I know she's your sister, but even you must admit she's a knockout."

"I do, but she's not a toy or a diversion." Damien's eyes narrowed in warning.

"I never thought she was." Nathan returned his cool gaze unflinchingly.

"Good," Damien said and nodded as he silently studied the other man. He thought they could become good friends but not if he did anything to harm his sister.

"I don't want to hurt Marcy," Nathan assured him, sensing Damien's thoughts.

"Then don't," Damien simply ordered.

"I don't plan on it," Nathan said, but even as he uttered the words, he knew that was a promise he might not be able to keep.

"Are you enjoying being back in New York?" Damien changed subjects, having said what he had needed to.

"Very much."

"After Tasha and I get settled in as an old married couple, we'll have to take you out and reintroduce you to some of the good spots," Damien offered.

"I'd like that." Nathan smiled.

Nathan's eyes connected with Marcy's again, and she smiled at him knowingly. He had a feeling she knew exactly what he and her brother were talking about, and she was going to make his resolve not to become involved with her near impossible to keep—just as he feared he was going to find it nearly impossible to live up to his promise to leave her alone.

Two and a half hours later the occupants of the private dining room were preparing to leave and go their separate ways. A few days later, they would all gather again for Damien and Natasha's wedding.

"Can I bum a ride home from someone?" Marcy glanced expectantly at Nathan. "My car's in the shop."

"Tasha and I can drop you off." Damien placed an affectionate arm around his sister's shoulders. "It's on the way."

"It is on Nathan's way, too," Nicole quickly intervened.

Marcy silently vowed to send her a huge bouquet of flowers the next day. She was turning out to be a wonderful ally.

"That's a fabulous idea," Linda decided, winking at Margaret. "Nathan, you take Marcy home."

"It's no problem. We can take her," Damien insisted, despite Marcy's glare.

Damien could see what was going on here, and though Marcy didn't seem to mind, he did; for some reason, even though he had spoken with Nathan and liked him, something was nagging him about Natasha's brother. In his gut—and he had learned from painful experiences to trust his gut—he knew that somehow Nathan was going to end up hurting his sister, and he would do everything in his power to stop that from happening.

"Darling, I'm tired and would rather go straight home," Natasha intervened. "Nathan, you don't mind taking Marcy home do you?"

Nathan realized every female present in the room was very skillfully ambushing him. He had come up against some worthy adversaries in his day but none as lethal as the quintuplet in front of him. What could one do against such skillful opponents, except surrender—and hope to live to fight another day?

"No, not at all," he dryly agreed.

"Good, now that is all settled." Linda smiled pleased and walked over to talk to Margaret. Marcy was a lovely woman and might be just what her absentee son needed to get him to settle down.

"You'd better watch out, son, your mother and Marcy's mother are plotting your downfall." Lincoln slapped his son on the back as Marcy walked away to retrieve her coat.

"Really? You could have fooled me, Dad." Nathan shook

his head in exasperation as he glanced at the smiling faces of the two women in question.

"Ready to go, Nathan?" Marcy came back with her leather coat draped over her arm.

"As I'll ever be," he muttered, taking her coat and placing it over her shoulders.

"What?" She glanced at him, stifling a laugh.

"Nothing," he denied. "Good night everyone," he shouted as they prepared to leave.

"Good night!" Marcy beamed as she preceded him out.

"Promising." Margaret approved, having witnessed her daughter's keen interest in Nathan on New Year's Eve manifested again tonight. Obviously, Marcy was serious, and after watching the two tonight, it was obvious Nathan was taken with Marcy, too. Although being a man, he was trying his best to fight it.

"Yes, I think you're right," Linda agreed as both women walked away to discuss their children's futures.

Nathan was silent for most of the drive, which was okay with her. She was formulating her strategy. He was so much work, but she knew he'd be worth it in the end. She would remind him of this one day, and they would laugh about him clinging to his overrated bacherlorhood.

When they reached her condo, he opened the car door and helped her out and then started to walk back around to the driver's side. She placed a restraining hand on his arm. "You're not going to leave me here, are you?"

"I was," he curtly agreed.

"Nathan, anyone could be lurking in the dark, just waiting for me. Then what would I do?" She feigned alarm. "I'd be helpless."

Despite his black mood, he smiled genuinely at her assertion. "Marcy, one thing you will never be is helpless."

"Oh, I don't know." She took his proffered arm as he walked her into the building. "I'm pretty helpless when it comes to you."

"Marcy." His steps faltered at her admission. "Don't say that."

"Why not? It's true." He was silent for the elevator ride to her floor. "Come in for a drink," she offered as she unlocked the door and stepped inside.

"No, I'd better not." He turned to leave.

"Come on in, I won't bite. I promise."

Before he knew what had hit him, he was pulled inside, and the door decisively clicked behind him. He knew all he had to do was leave, but as was becoming a habit with Marcy, he gave in because he wanted to. Her apartment was spacious, decorated in pastels with a tapestry sofa and chairs.

"Your place is very nice." He took off his coat in resignation.

"Thanks. Make yourself at home," she yelled, throwing her coat over a chair as she walked into what he assumed was the kitchen, returning seconds later with a bottle of white wine and two glasses. "Will you do the honors?"

"Sure." He wanted to protest but decided against it. He would have one glass and then go.

"Sit down," she said as she motioned to the sofa and as he complied, sat closely beside him holding glasses out to him, which he filled before placing the bottle onto the table.

"I can't stay long, Marcy." He thought it best to get that out before she got any ideas in her beautiful head.

"We'll see."

He tasted his wine. "This is good."

"Very," she whispered, taking a sip of the cold liquid before placing her still-full glass on the table. "You're so buff." She lightly fingered his biceps and shoulders. "I've never met a lawyer in such great shape."

"I enjoy working out." He grabbed her hand, halting her disturbing exploration.

"Mmm," she approved, trailing the fingers of her free hand across his broad chest. "I can tell."

"Marcy…"

"What?" She stared into his conflicted eyes.

When he failed to answer, she leaned across the sofa, took his glass from his unresisting fingers and placed it on the table beside hers. Then framing his face in her hands, she kissed him. She felt the tension in him as he resisted her and himself, but within seconds, his lips changed from cold and stiff to warm and caressing—though he refrained from touching her. She tasted the wine on his lips—and the barely restrained passion.

"I've wanted to do that all day," she murmured, pulling slightly back, though her mouth was still in close proximity to his.

Turbulent, dangerous eyes bore into hers before lowering to focus on her incredibly soft lips that tasted of wine, honey and dangerous desire. He knew he should push her away and leave; instead he reached out, pulled her closer and let his mouth ravage hers. Out of control, impatient hands focused on the buttons of her jacket until it was completely undone, and then he pulled her down to lie beside him as he reclined back onto the sofa.

When his wandering hands slipped beneath the undone jacket folds, he realized to his delight and dismay that she was only wearing a thin black lace teddy, which covered next to nothing of the satiny skin underneath. He rolled until she was nearly lying beneath him. His hands caressed her lace-covered breasts and stomach as his mouth left hers to blaze a trail across her neck and collarbone to the swell of a breast.

His hot tongue licked out and tasted a nipple, which he felt harden through the chemise. With a groan, his mouth opened warmly, taking the still-covered swell into his mouth and suckled maddeningly until she thought she would shatter. Her hands moved behind his head as he continued to feast on her flesh through the now-wet fabric she prayed he would rip away as he was ripping away any sense of sanity she possessed.

In the back of his mind, a nagging voice reminding him of his promise to remain emotionally unattached while he was in Black Ops; the type of life he led wasn't easy—in fact, it could be downright brutal. He couldn't become involved with Marcy; it wasn't fair to her. She deserved better than he could give her, and he knew that.

With a mind of their own, his hand snaked under the satin to touch the warm, silky skin of her stomach, and he felt her fingers clutch the back of his head and release. Desire built within him almost to the point of no return. If he touched her a second longer, if he felt her trembling against him another minute, he would take her and damn the consequences. Somehow, using willpower years of training had instilled, he pulled away and sat up.

It took her a few seconds to realize he was no longer lying next to her or touching her. When she did, she opened cloudy eyes and slowly sat up beside him.

"Stay." She sighed as she placed her arms around his neck, realizing he meant to leave her and himself unfulfilled.

"You've just met me," he hoarsely responded, fighting for control that was rapidly escaping him.

"We've known each other for a week," she reminded.

"Barely a week," he contradicted.

"I feel as if I've known you all my life." She scraped her teeth maddeningly along his jaw before lifting her head to stare into his darkening eyes. "Don't you want me?"

"Marcy, a man would have to be crazy not to want you." He nearly groaned. But then he forced himself to add, "But I'm here to see my family, not to start a relationship with you—with anyone."

He reluctantly disentangled her arms from his neck, stood and quickly walked to the door.

"Nathan?" Her soft, seductive voice halted him.

"What?" He asked without turning around. God he wanted her; had he ever wanted anything this much?

"You know what they say about making plans?" He turned to face her, but neither of them made a move toward the other.

"No, what?" At the moment, he didn't know his name or how he was articulating at all.

"The best laid ones go to waste," she responded with a smile. Silently vowing she would make sure his did. Impulsively, she walked over, cupped his face between her hands and kissed him again.

"Marcy, would you let me take the initiative for once?" he asked against her lips.

"I'd love to. Go ahead," she ordered, pulling slightly back.

He shook his head and smiled down at her, "Would you like to go out to dinner with me tomorrow night?" *What the...? Why had he asked that?*

"I'd love to." She beamed. "That was very nicely done."

"Thank you." He silently berated himself for his lack of discipline where she was concerned.

"What time?" Her eyes memorized every curve of his handsome face.

"Seven." He committed himself to his unwise course

of action, and unable to help himself, he began outlining her face with his fingertips. She shuddered at his touch.

"Should I meet you, or would you rather pick me up?" she docilely asked, breath coming in trembling gasps.

"I'll pick you up," he nearly whispered as the fingers of his other hand played with loose strands of her hair; it was so soft, so incredibly soft.

"How should I dress? Casual? After five? Elegant?"

She couldn't believe she could comprehend let alone formulate questions. He was touching her lightly yet urgently. She was a quivering mass of jelly, yet somehow she still stood before him instead of sinking bonelessly to the floor at his feet.

"Elegantly," he decided and said as his hands followed her example and cupped her face.

"Mmm, sounds nice." She shakily smiled. "You take charge very well."

"Thanks." Intense eyes stared into hers, and he decided to take even more as he placed a hand behind her nape and pulled her irresistible lips to his.

Devastation. No other word described what he did to her with that kiss—or what she did to him. He could happily feast on those lips for an eternity. She gladly clung to his hard shoulders as his mouth continued to plunder. When his lips released hers, they were both breathing hard. She opened stormy eyes to see the echoing depths of his.

"Very well indeed," she murmured. "That was a wonderful first kiss."

He frowned. "That wasn't our first kiss. New Year's Eve was."

"New Year's Eve I kissed you." She smiled impishly. "This is the first time you've initiated a kiss between us. I hope it won't be the last."

"If you recall, I kissed you back on New Year's Eve—"

he traced the outline of her trembling lips with his fingers "—and I thoroughly enjoyed it."

"You did?"

"Oh, you know I did," he said and smiled.

"So did I. Let's not wait so long before you kiss me again," she softly suggested.

"We'll see." He touched her trembling lips with his fingers and then quickly removed them. "Good night, Marcy."

"Good night," she echoed. "Thanks for bringing me home."

He glanced back at her trying to decide what he should do and what he wanted to do next—his head won out over want, and he determinedly opened the door and left. If he touched her again, he would be lost.

When her limbs would finally obey her commands, Marcy slowly retraced her steps and fell across the sofa. She let out her breath with a long, unsteady sigh. Gingerly, fingers touched her lips, and starry eyes closed as she remembered the feel of Nathan's lips, body and his heart beating so close to hers.

She'd had a few crushes in her day but nothing close to what she felt for Nathan. She felt alive with him; he did things to her mind and spirit that she had never experienced before. They hadn't known each other long, but he was the one; she knew it. Now her goal was to make him realize she was the one for him.

Chapter 3

The next night, Marcy and Nathan sat in the private dining room at one of the most expensive restaurants in town. Fresh roses of every imaginable color were scattered throughout the room in one arrangement or another. A bouquet of red ones sat beside her plate on the table. Soft, romantic music was being piped into the room, and the light was dim. The flames of candles danced in the table centerpieces.

She silently admitted that when he took charge, he took charge well. She had dressed as instructed in an elegant gold sequined floor-length gown with a slit up one side to her midthigh. The halter top left her back, shoulders and arms bare. Her hair was left down, cascading over her shoulders to her back in soft curls. The body of the gown fit her like a glove, accentuating her female curves in all the right places. Nathan wore a black designer suit that hung on him as if it had been especially made for him.

The evening passed in a perfectly wonderful blur. All she was certain of was that she was having a wonderful time with a secretive and oh-so-alluring man whose company she craved.

"How am I doing?" he asked as they finished their dinner.

"Excellently," she vowed.

"Dance with me," he commanded, taking her hand and pulling her up into his arms.

"Mmm, beyond compare." She amended her previous statement as she rested her head on his sturdy shoulder, and her fingers entwined with his.

"I'm glad you approve," he whispered against her ear.

She felt and heard him inhale her fragrance, and a smile curved her lips as the hand on her waist pulled her closer still. He ran his mouth softly up and down the crook of her neck, creating shivers of anticipation within her.

"I definitely approve," she whispered.

"You have beautiful hair." Raising his head, he slowly ran fingers through its length from root to tip several times.

"You have my mother to thank for that."

"How so?"

"She refused to let anything touch my hair that wasn't natural, which meant no chemicals at all." She paused and laughed impishly. "That is until I took it upon myself to perm it."

He smiled and asked, "What did your mother do?"

"Let's just say Daddy and Dami had to protect me for a few weeks." She chuckled at the memory.

"How old were you?"

"Twenty."

"A mere baby who couldn't possibly make such a decision," Nathan teased.

"Mom will always think of me as her little girl." Marcy sighed in angst, and they shared a comfortable laugh.

"Well, remind me to thank your mother next time I see her."

"Mmm," she said and sighed. "I will." She moved a little closer to him. "You can thank me, too. Right now."

She wanted him to kiss her, and she wasn't disappointed as his mouth swooped down and seduced hers. He lingered over the kiss, savoring her different tastes and textures. She met the probing inquisitiveness of his lips, content just to have him go on kissing her; however, when his hot tongue darted into her mouth in a search for hers, she wanted nothing more than a molten combination of their bodies and hearts.

The kiss changed from gentle to hungry as he set out to plunder and destroy. Never before had a woman nearly caused him to take her on the spot with just a kiss, but he was close to doing just that with Marcy; every time he touched her, he lost his grip on sanity. His hands ran up her silky bare back, molding her, pressing her closer to his rock-hard length.

How had he ended up kissing her? He didn't remember. His moves had been instinctive, automatic—as was his hunger for her; it was a hunger so intense that it nearly made him pull her to the floor, strip away their clothes and fuse his body with hers. What was she doing to him? What would she do if he didn't continue to fight her and himself?

"We could go back to my place," she achingly suggested as he slowly released her lips.

"Will you let me be the man?" He groaned, nibbling at her mouth, forgetting his resolve to push her away.

Despite the desire racing through her, she laughed at his tone, which quickly turned to a moan at his actions.

"Honey, you're definitely a man." To prove her point, she pressed tighter against him.

He whispered, "You're killing me."

"I'm sorry," she shakily apologized, running her lips along his strong jaw.

"No, you're not," he accused with a smile.

She batted her eyes innocently. "I am, truly."

His heart thudded against his chest, beating frantically in concert with hers. One hand ran down her back to her hip, anchoring her lower body against his.

"I've never met a woman like you." He marveled while his other hand threaded through her thick locks, pulling her head back.

"And you never will again," she promised, and he silently concurred.

"God, I love your hair."

His hand fisted in the silky tresses as he imagined it sliding across his stomach while her lips and tongue caressed him. He grew harder as the welcomed image assailed his overheated senses.

"I've thought about cutting it," she admitted on a sigh, her hands resting on his broad shoulders.

"Don't. Don't ever," he ordered, finally pulling her lips back to his.

"I won't," she promised into his mouth.

For several long minutes, she was in heaven. For a few agonizing seconds, he surrendered. His mouth demanded nothing less than complete capitulation from hers, which she was happy to give for a few seconds before aggressively participating in their heated, carnal duel of lips and tongues.

"You are so beautiful," he nearly growled as he forced his mouth away from hers.

"And you're very handsome," she reciprocated, partially opening her dazed eyes to gaze at him.

"You're a hard woman to resist," he reluctantly admitted as he sampled those sweet lips of hers once again for a few long moments.

"Stop trying," she softly suggested. "Are you going to take me home?"

"Yes," he readily agreed, slowly releasing her.

He was damning his soul to hell, but so be it. He held out his hand to her; she gladly took it, and they walked out.

Thank the Lord for the ride home in the car. It afforded him time to come to his senses, cleared his head and stopped him from making a monumental mistake. Marcy was special, and she deserved a hell of a lot better than he was able to give her. He had promised himself and her brother that he wouldn't hurt her, but if he did as his body cried out for him to do and made wonderful love to her tonight, he would be on course to do just that.

Marcy turned her head to stare at Nathan's intense profile. His hands gripped the steering wheel tightly, and his brow was furrowed in concentration. Uh-oh, he was thinking, and instinctively, she knew she wouldn't like the conclusion he had evidently come to.

Finally, the car stopped outside of her apartment. He helped her out, and they walked through the cold night air into the building. The ride in the elevator was silent, confirming her earlier suspicion that he was rethinking his decision to stay with her tonight. They got off on her floor, and she unlocked the door and stepped inside waiting for him to do the same.

"I'm not coming in, Marcy." He proved her fears to be correct.

"But, I thought…" Her voice trailed off.

"I know."

"The drive gave you time to think, didn't it?" She smiled slightly despite her obvious disappointment.

"Yes, thankfully," he admitted.

"Why thankfully?" she murmured, debating whether or not to make him forget his newfound resolve.

"We're moving way too fast," he remarked, shoving his hands in his jacket pockets to keep from touching her, and she smiled at his actions. *She doesn't miss anything.*

"Yes, we are moving fast," she agreed.

"That's not what I expected you to say." He somberly studied her gorgeous face.

"Maybe this is." She paused before continuing. "We're moving fast but not too fast. I'm not trying to pass some time with you Nathan. I don't want a brief affair," she confessed.

"I'd be disappointed if you were or did."

A brief affair was all he had to offer, and it wasn't what he wanted with her. She desired stability, permanency and roots—none of those things had a place in his life right now, which is why he had no place in hers.

"What are you thinking?" She leaned against the door and smiled at him thoughtfully. "What do *you* want, Nathan?"

He remained silent as he pondered her question. It wasn't that he couldn't tell her what he wanted; it was that he didn't dare. He wanted her—not just for a night but for dozens of nights, endless nights.

"Good night, Marcy." He valiantly fought not to kiss her and somehow succeeded. Quickly turning, he walked toward the elevator.

"You didn't answer my question," she called after him, and he turned to somberly face her.

"I know," he agreed before the elevator doors closed.

"Damn," she whispered as a smile played about her lips. She didn't understand why he was bent on ignoring the attraction between them, but she was just as adamant that he wouldn't succeed. "This makes two times, and it's the last time I allow you to walk out on me, Mr. Carter," she promised with a determined smile as she closed the door.

Two days later, Natasha walked down the aisle and married Marcy's brother. Marcy had never seen either of them look happier and had never been happier for them. Natasha had been a beautiful bride in the dress Nicole designed. The tiny waist accentuated her figure; the full skirt was reminiscent of southern belles, and moved as though it was a part of her. Satin bows trailed down the back of the gown. Her shoulders were left bare. Her hair was pinned up, and a crystal tiara was the crowning glory, attached to a cathedral-length veil.

Damien and all the groomsmen, which included Nathan, were dressed in black tuxedos. Marcy had glanced at him more than once during the ceremony, and she had felt him glance at her. Her eyes searched the room and found Nathan standing with Nicole and their father on the other side of the ballroom. Determinedly, Marcy walked across to spirit him away. They hadn't really been alone all evening, though she had finagled it so that he was the one who escorted her down the aisle. She ached to be held in his arms; it was time to get Mr. Carter on the dance floor.

"I don't think Nathan has a chance." Natasha's eyes moved from Marcy to focus on her new husband, whose arms she was dancing in.

"I think you're right," Damien agreed, also refocusing his eyes on his new bride.

"How do you feel about that?" Natasha watched him closely.

"I like Nathan."

"But?"

"But I'm worried about Marcy," he confessed.

"Nathan would never hurt her," she positively responded.

"I know that," he said more for her benefit than actual belief.

"Do you?"

"Yes." He kissed her hard and then to prove he wasn't worried glanced at their mothers and joked, "He has powerful forces working against him."

"He does indeed. Momma has met a kindred spirit in your mother." She smiled as her eyes drifted over the two women both dressed in varying shades of lavender.

"Poor Nathan. I feel sorry for him," Damien sympathized.

"I wouldn't. They make a stunning couple," Natasha asserted.

"Natasha, no matchmaking," he ordered. "Our mothers are bad enough."

"I'm just saying—" Her words were muffled against his mouth as he kissed her thoroughly.

"I don't want to think or talk about anyone except you and me, wife." He kissed her lips again lingeringly until she was clinging to his shoulders and could think of nothing except how much she wanted to be alone with him.

"Neither do I, husband," she agreed, winding her arms around his neck as he slowly twirled her around the dance floor.

"I love you with all my heart," he vowed, their bodies barely moving now.

"I love you more," she whispered.

"Thank you for putting up with me, Tasha," he replied, pulling her closer.

"Any time." She smiled and pulled his lips back down to hers.

Marcy and Nicole were dressed similarly in formal attire consisting of black velvet A-line dresses, off the shoulder, with a slit up the back allowing for ease of movement. In her hands, Marcy held the bridal bouquet she had caught. The garter Nathan had caught was secured around her thigh. She smiled as she recalled the way she had teased him as he had reluctantly placed it there amid cheers and whistles.

"Hello, everyone." Marcy beamed as she approached Nathan, his sister and father.

"Marcy, I haven't had a chance to tell you how lovely you look," Lincoln replied, kissing her cheek.

"Thank you, Lincoln," she smiled at him. "Your daughter did a fabulous job on the gowns on such short notice."

"It was a labor of love," Nicole replied. "Momma is motioning to you." She touched her father's arm, and he looked in the direction she pointed.

"Ah, what is that woman up to now?" He rolled his eyes heavenward and walked away chuckling.

"Are you enjoying yourself, Nathan?" Marcy touched his arm lightly. She felt his muscles tense up at the contact.

"It's a great party." He cursed his eyes for lingering on her kissable full red lips.

"I could use some champagne." Feeling like a fifth wheel, Nicole prepared to leave them alone.

"I'll get it," Nathan quickly offered.

"No, stay and entertain Marcy. I'll get it." Nicole smiled at him, winked at Marcy and then quickly disappeared.

"Aren't they a beautiful couple?" Marcy grabbed his hand and pulled him onto the dance floor.

"Yes." Nathan eyed her suspiciously. "What are you and my sister up to?"

"Whatever do you mean?" Marcy feigned innocence while moving into his arms.

She was exasperating—but intriguing and oh, so desirable. If things were different, he would be pursuing her instead of the other way around, but things *weren't* different.

"You can pull me a little closer, Nathan. I won't break," she instructed as they began to dance.

"If you recall, I do know how to dance with a woman." Despite his better judgment, he pulled her closer, anyway—the way he had danced with her the other night.

He had purposefully avoided her since their dinner together. Time apart had done nothing to squelch his desire for her. Instead, it had only intensified to near-crippling proportions, yet it had reminded him of the many reasons he shouldn't and couldn't become involved with her. But now that he was touching her again, none of them seemed very important.

"Mmm, that's better." She sighed, fingers tightening on his shoulder. "Why are you being so standoffish today? The other night you willingly held me close and kissed me."

"Yes, I know," he admitted, wishing he could forget about that.

"You told me you thought I was beautiful. Didn't you mean it?"

"Yes, you're very beautiful," he grudgingly replied.

"You don't have to sound so resentful about it," she chided, and despite himself, he laughed. "That's much better," she approved.

"Marcy, I really can't become involved with you." His

words were deadly serious, though he continued to smile at her.

"Why not?"

"It's not a good time for me." He nearly groaned the words as she moved closer to him and slid her arm up until her fingers rested at the nape of his neck.

"We can't choose when we'll meet someone who excites and captivates us," she whispered, eyes darkening at his nearness.

"I know. I wish we could." He stopped himself from tasting those soft sweet lips somehow.

"So you wouldn't be attracted to me?"

"Yes," he agreed, and she smiled at him.

"Nicole says you'll be here for about a month?"

"More or less."

"Well, I'm giving you fair warning that while you're here, I plan on monopolizing your time."

"Don't I have any say in the matter?"

She appeared to consider his question and then smiled. "No, not really."

His somber expression disappeared, and he laughed. "You're pretty aggressive."

"As you should know by now, I don't believe in wasting time when I see something I want," she easily responded.

"And what do you want?"

"Only your heart," she simply replied.

"Is that all?" He smiled again despite himself.

"Yes, that's all," she acquiesced. "And I promise you it won't be painful. In fact, if you relax, you might actually enjoy falling in love with me," she boldly suggested.

"Are you trying to tell me that you're in love with me?" He stared at her aghast.

"Very close to it," she admitted.

"We haven't known each other long enough for you to

be anywhere near in love with me," he contradicted her. Though inwardly he was flattered and humbled by her words.

"Don't tell me how I feel," she softly ordered. "Besides, what does time have to do with affairs of the heart? My father fell in love with my mother in hours. My brother fell in love with your sister in days, and your mother and father fell in love at first sight."

He raised an eyebrow. "How do you know how long it took my father and mother to fall in love?"

"I asked them."

"You what?" That's all he needed—her feeding his mother's incessant need to play matchmaker.

"I asked them," she softly reiterated. "They're lovely people. Your entire family is wonderful."

"Thank you. So is yours."

"You don't know what to make of me, do you?" She smiled a dazzling smile that nearly brought him to his knees.

"No, not at all," he readily agreed.

"Don't worry, I'll teach you," she promised, moving closer in his arms until he couldn't tell where he ended and she began.

She felt too good next to him; her body fit perfectly against his. The exotic perfume she insisted on wearing was killing him; this was laughable—a highly trained soldier was rendered helpless by perfume and the formidable woman who wore it.

Not knowing what to say, he remained silent; however, his shocked expression spoke volumes. Marcy continued smiling at him as he twirled her around the dance floor. He had been on many dangerous assignments through the years, yet he feared none would compare to the danger Marcy Johnson posed to his longing heart.

Chapter 4

Nicole and Nathan sat finishing up their lunch at a downtown Manhattan restaurant. Having just seen her at Damien and Natasha's wedding a few days ago, he had been a little surprised to receive her invitation but was always happy to spend time with his little sister. However, it soon became apparent that she had more on her mind than just catching up; she was on a fishing expedition, and he had a pretty good idea for whom.

"I'm glad you invited me to lunch today, sis." Nathan smiled as she sampled her chocolate cream pie.

"So am I." Nicole licked whipped cream from her fork.

Nathan grinned. "You seem to be enjoying your dessert much more than you did your main course."

"Raw fish—raw anything—is not my idea of food." Nicole placed a hand to her stomach at the memory, and Nathan laughed.

"You're the one who said you wanted to try something new." He shrugged. "I thought you'd like sushi."

"I should have known better than to let you choose the restaurant." Nicole accusingly pointed her fork at him. "Remember how you loved using me as your guinea pig when we were little?"

"Hey, you always pestered me to sample my cooking."

"That's not *exactly* the way I remember it. I should have been suspicious when you covered it in chocolate to tempt me to taste it." They shared a laugh. "Those were good times, weren't they?"

"The best." Nathan squeezed her hand. "I've missed you."

"I've missed you, too." Nicole returned his smile and then grew serious. "What have you been doing for four long years away from home, Nathan?"

"Just working, trying to build a life for myself," he noncommittally replied.

"Have you?"

He shrugged. "I guess so."

"Don't you want someone to share it with?"

"I don't have the time or the inclination for a lasting relationship." He took a sip of his coffee. "I'm perfectly happy with my life the way it is."

"Mmm," Nicole whispered, eyeing him over the rim of her cup.

He knew she didn't believe him. Hell, he didn't believe himself—especially since meeting Marcy.

"Anyway, I don't want to talk about me. Tell me about you," he invited.

"I'm going to Paris as a junior associate for Alexander James at the beginning of March. Momma doesn't want me to go, but she's been very supportive as has Dad."

"I don't know who Alexander James is, but I'm very proud of you." Nathan smiled.

"He owns one of the biggest fashion houses in Europe," she laughingly informed him. "Thank you for being proud of me."

"What about your love life? Are you seeing anyone? I expected to have to threaten at least ten men with bodily harm when I got home," he teased.

"You're safe on that front," she said and laughed. "There's no one special in my life—yet."

"Yet? Does that mean you have someone in mind?"

"No, but I do plan to fall in love and get married some-day," she solemnly vowed.

"You say it so easily." He envied her.

"Of course I do. What's to be afraid of?" She frowned slightly at his tone. "Is that why you're pushing Marcy away, because you're afraid of commitment?" She skill-fully steered the conversation back to where she wanted it to be.

"No, I'm not." He took a bite of his pie. "Maybe I just don't like her."

Nicole laughed in disbelief. "You looked as if you liked her very well a few days ago at the wedding."

"I was just being nice," he insisted.

"Of course you were." Nicole chuckled when her obvi-ous disbelief at Nathan's previous statement was met with a frown from him. "So, have you seen her since then?"

"No, why would I?" At her amused expression, he nearly growled, "I wish everyone would stop trying to marry me off to Marcy Johnson. We've just met."

"That's true," Nicole agreed. Then she quickly added, "But you two make such a striking pair. Don't you think she's attractive?"

"She's beautiful," he admitted, noisily placing his fork on his plate. *Here we go,* he sighed inwardly.

"Don't you have fun when you're with her?"

"She irritates me," he quickly asserted—too quickly.

"All the better." Nicole smiled as she sipped her coffee.

"Nicole…" he started, but her cell phone ringing interrupted him.

"Sorry. I meant to turn this thing off." She retrieved her phone from her purse. "Hello?" She paused listening. "Funny you should call, Nathan and I were just talking about you." She paused again before chuckling. "We're having lunch. Mmm-hmm. Yes, of course he is." Nicole smiled at him and then laughed.

"If you're going to discuss me over the phone, have the decency to do it in private." He frowned when she waved her hand at him in dismissal.

"Yes, that was him," Nicole affirmed around a chuckle. "I'd love to. I'll stop by your office after lunch, around one-thirty? Okay? Yes, just a moment." She handed him the phone.

"I don't want to talk to her," he refused, retreating as if it were a poisonous snake.

"Are you so afraid of Marcy that you can't even speak to her on the phone?" Nicole goaded, and he reluctantly took the phone from her.

"Yes?" He spoke curtly into the receiver. "No… I… If you… How can I answer if you keep hurling questions at me?" He sighed in frustration. "No, I'm not in a bad mood."

"You could have fooled me," Nicole whispered, taking another bite of her pie as he glared at her.

"I haven't decided yet. No, I… Hello?" He cursed under his breath and handed her the phone back.

"Is she gone?" Nicole hid a smile.

"Yes, way gone."

"What did she want?" She placed the phone in her bag.

"She invited me to dinner with her parents tonight." He sighed heavily, taking another drink of his coffee, suddenly wishing it was whiskey.

"Are you going to go?"

"She hung up before I could refuse." He scratched his chin, which he always did when he was frustrated.

"Good for her." Nicole grinned when she received another scowl. "Nathan, if you keep frowning like that, you'll frighten away any woman who might potentially be interested in you," she wisely advised.

"It doesn't seem to work with Marcy."

"Well, Marcy isn't any woman," Nicole unnecessarily informed him.

"Meaning?"

"Meaning I don't think you'll easily frighten her away." Nicole placed the last piece of her pie into her mouth.

"Is that what you think I'm trying to do?"

"Aren't you?" she countered, raising an eyebrow.

"I just don't have time for a serious relationship right now," he evaded.

"So you admit if you allowed yourself to you could have something serious with Marcy," she inferred.

"Will you stop twisting my words around?" he angrily hissed.

"They're your words and feelings, not mine." Nicole reached across the table to touch his fisted hand. "Nathan, I love you," she whispered in a voice she knew always made him putty in her hands.

"I love you, too, you traitor." He smiled as he brought her hand to his lips.

"You know we all just want to see you happy," she continued and he sighed.

"I know that," he admitted. "How would you feel if two families were interfering in your personal life?"

"I wouldn't like it." Before he could respond, she continued. "But there comes a time when you have to give in to fate."

"And what is my fate? To be with Marcy Johnson?"

"A lot of people seem to think so."

He sighed. "Doesn't it matter what I think?"

"Of course it does, but for some reason, you're fighting your feelings for Marcy, and that's why everyone else feels obligated to get involved," she wisely asserted.

"Maybe I don't feel anything for her," he lied, and received a disbelieving look that would have done their mother proud.

"If you truly meant that, everyone would back off," she softly informed him.

"I do mean it," he firmly stated, replacing his credit card in his wallet when the waiter returned it to him.

"No, you don't," she softly contradicted. "Your mouth says you don't want her in your life, but when the two of you are together, your eyes, your body and your demeanor all say something else."

"Well, I'm just an open book, aren't I?" He didn't try to hide his annoyance at her intuitiveness.

"No, quite the contrary. You're a mystery, and in case you didn't know, women love solving mysteries," she advised and stood. "Thank you for lunch…even though you made me eat sushi." She punched his arm playfully as he stood, and they walked out of the restaurant.

"You're welcome, even though I had to listen to unsolicited advice." He pulled a strand of her hair in retaliation.

"Be glad it was from me and not from Momma or Mrs. Johnson," she informed, placing on her gloves.

"Oh, I am." He rolled his eyes heavenward at the thought.

"Do you want me to give Marcy a message?" She paused and added purposefully, "Or would you like to tag along?"

"No to both questions," he sarcastically declined. "Tell the folks I will be out to the house in a few days."

"Better sooner than later or Momma will come gunning for you." Nicole kissed his cheek, and then she was off.

As he watched her weave through the busy streets, he pondered her wise words. For one so young, she was very intuitive and just as annoying. He smiled lovingly as she disappeared around a corner—a smile that metamorphosed into a self-derisive sneer as he realized he did want to go with her so that he could see that tenacious, gorgeously seductive Marcy Johnson again.

Nathan glanced at his uneasy expression in the mirror as he finished knotting his gray-and-black tie. Satisfied, he turned away and returned to the bedroom, sitting down on the bed as he donned his black leather shoes before standing and putting on his charcoal-gray suit jacket.

He just didn't want to be rude—that was the reason he had accepted Marcy's dinner invitation. He wasn't the least bit excited that he would be spending the evening with her. He placed a white handkerchief in his breast pocket and took his black wool coat out of the closet.

He was just being a gentleman like his mother had always taught him to be. He'd have dinner with her parents, come home and would never see or think about Marcy again. That's what he'd do, he resolutely decided, and then he laughed bitterly.

Who did he think he was kidding? He couldn't wait to see her, to smell that wicked perfume she insisted on wearing just to drive him mad, to touch that soft satiny skin and taste her luscious lips. *How the hell had this happened?* He had come home for a visit with his family, and all he had seemed to accomplish was to get tangled up with a charming, beautiful she-devil whose very name made his blood boil, and the more he saw her, the more intrigued and ensnared he became.

He *needed* to stay away from her. It shouldn't be so hard to make that happen; then why was that simple task next to impossible for him to accomplish? He knew what he had to do, yet even as he picked up the phone to cancel their *date* he hesitated because despite knowing right from wrong, he wanted to see Marcy tonight. *You can't start anything with her, Nathan, so make the phone call and cancel!* Before he could dial her number—which he was annoyed at himself for memorizing—someone knocked on the door, and he walked over to answer it.

"Hi, handsome." Marcy touched his arm as she leaned over and kissed his lips lightly but long enough to make him nearly groan.

As always, she looked stunning in a midnight-blue dress that reached her calves. Though the majority of the dress was hidden by her cream-colored wool coat, what he was able to glimpse accentuated her feminine curves splendidly.

"Marcy, I was just about to call you…" His voice trailed off when he inhaled the sultry perfume she always wore, which fogged his head.

"To cancel, no doubt." She threw her bag on a table and smiled at his shocked expression.

"Why would you think that?" She laughed a carefree sound that ripped through him and made him want to crush his mouth to those curved rose-colored lips.

"A little birdie told me," she whispered, picking her bag up again. "Are you ready to go?"

"I suppose." He didn't sound at all enthused.

"Nathan, it's only dinner with my parents." She made it sound so innocent when he knew nothing could be further from the truth.

"Is it?" He pulled on his coat and opened the door following her out.

"What else would it be?" she sweetly asked as they walked to the elevator.

"An ambush," he muttered under his breath as he followed her. She turned and chuckled at him leaving little doubt that she had heard his dire prediction.

They were all gathered at the dinner table an hour later. Nathan had to admit he was enjoying himself. Marcy's parents reminded him of his; they obviously loved each other and their daughter very much. Now more than ever sitting around the table with them, he could see himself as a part of Marcy's world, which is what he imagined she had in mind when she invited him tonight.

Her mother and Nathan talked avidly about the law. She learned that he had practiced criminal and corporate law and really preferred corporate. Marcy listened to the two of them talk over statutes and briefs. She sat back and enjoyed herself. Her mother got more out of him about his work in twenty minutes than she had been able to accomplish in a week or so.

"Nathan, if you decide in the near future to relocate back to New York—" she glanced pointedly at her daughter and then back to him "—there's an opening in my firm. I'd be happy to put in a good word for you."

Michael shook his head at his wife. She was really laying it on thick.

"Thank you, Mrs. Johnson. That's very kind of you." Nathan felt the ropes that had been carefully lassoed around him once he walked in the door beginning to tighten.

"I'm not just being kind. I mean it. We could use another bright attorney," she emphasized. "I'm working on this case now that's very challenging."

For the next few minutes, Nathan was happy to engage in intense legal talk with Margaret. At least while talking shop, she wasn't prying into his personal life.

Marcy smiled at her father. He shook his head, and she chuckled, causing Nathan and Margaret's eyes to refocus on them.

"Sweetie, do you have the feeling you're in the middle of a *Perry Mason* episode?" Michael winked at her from across the table.

"Yes, one of the more perplexing ones," Marcy agreed.

"Uh-oh, Nathan. I think they're not so subtly trying to tell us to lay off the lawyer talk." Margaret chuckled.

"No, you two go ahead. Dad and I will just start talking about the Dow Jones, NASDAQ, interest rates and—"

"No, please!" Margaret held up her hands in defeat and everyone laughed. "When we usually get together they outnumber me, so that's all I hear about," she moaned, raising her eyes heavenward.

"Ah, I see," Nathan sympathized.

"Don't get us wrong. We're very supportive about each other's careers." Michael grasped his wife's hand, and she smiled at him, nodding in agreement.

"We just don't understand a thing the other says when we start talking work," Margaret concluded and motioned to the food-laden table, "Nathan, can I get you anything else?"

"No, thank you, Mrs. Johnson. Dinner was delicious, but I'm stuffed."

"Thank you, but compliments go to Michael." She proudly kissed his cheek. "I am banned from the kitchen, much to my relief."

"My compliments, sir." Nathan chuckled and glanced at him.

"Thank you, son," Michael said and smiled.

"That clam chowder tasted just like my mother's," Nathan marveled.

"It should. It was her recipe." Michael laughed.

Nathan's eyes widened in shock. "She gave you *her* recipe?"

"They swapped dozens of them at our pre-New Year's party." Marcy smiled.

"She must like you very much. She guards her recipes with her life," Nathan seriously replied.

"We hit it off," Michael agreed. "All four of us have become good friends, and your mother and Margaret... well, let's just say that they have similar *hobbies*." He then winked at his wife.

"Really, Michael!" Margaret rapped his hand lightly. Nathan, who was beginning to relax, now seemed a little more tense thanks to her husband's ill-timed words. She would get him for this later.

"How much longer will you be in New York, Nathan?" Margaret tactfully changed the subject.

"Two or three weeks." He lowered his coffee cup.

"And then it's back to Washington?" Margaret folded her napkin and placed it on the tabletop, eyes intently focused on him.

"Yes, ma'am. Back to work."

"Unless a reason to stay presents itself." She glanced at her daughter.

Nathan cleared his throat. "I'm due back on time and can't prolong my vacation."

"Well—" Margaret smiled knowingly "—never say never, Nathan."

"Yes, ma'am." Nathan thought it best to keep his response short.

"What about your personal life?" Margaret single-mindedly continued with her seemingly innocent questions, and Nathan felt the noose tighten a little bit more. "Is there a special woman in Washington?"

"Mother." Marcy feigned outrage.

"What?" Margaret arched an eyebrow. "Is it a state secret?"

"No, of course not." Nathan shifted uncomfortably. "I...I don't have much of a personal life," he admitted and then realized his mistake.

"Well, that's a shame." Margaret frowned in disbelief. "A handsome man like you?"

Marcy's shoulders shook with laughter. She hid a smile behind her napkin and skillfully avoided Nathan's pointed gaze.

"My job keeps me pretty busy," Nathan offered, rubbing his chin. He saw where Marcy got her tenacity.

Michael shook his head as he watched his wife skillfully pump Nathan for information. She hadn't made partner for nothing; she had an unsurpassed knack of finding out what she wanted to know. Poor Nathan was finding that out firsthand.

"All work and no play, Nathan," Margaret chided. "What you need is a special woman in your life." She paused and glanced from him to her daughter and came to the point she had been dancing around all evening. "I think that you and our Marcy—"

"Margaret Johnson, will you stop browbeating Nathan," Michael softly, but firmly, interrupted his wife.

"I was doing no such thing," Margaret indignantly responded. "I was simply trying—"

"To do what, dear? Keep the conversation lively?" Michael's eyes twinkled with merriment.

She narrowed her eyes in warning. "Really, Michael!"

"It's quite all right," Nathan interjected, not wanting to start an argument.

Marcy touched his arm and shook her head negatively. She was smiling, so apparently everything was fine.

"You see?" Margaret glared at her husband. "Nathan wasn't offended. He understands what I was trying to do."

"Yes, I do," Nathan dryly agreed. He glanced at Marcy, who was being noticeably quiet; she smiled innocently at him—that little devil.

"Why don't we go into the living room for a drink?" Michael suggested. "I promise to try and curb my wife's curiosity."

"I will deal with you later, Michael Johnson," Margaret promised, and her husband smiled at the angry glint in her eyes, which only infuriated her more.

Where was Linda when she needed her? No one was being the least bit helpful. Nathan was skillfully evasive, Marcy was being understandably quiet and watchful and Michael—well, as she had promised, she would certainly deal with him later.

Chapter 5

"Your poor father." Nathan spoke mainly to break the silence as he weeded through traffic several hours later. Marcy had been uncharacteristically silent since leaving her parents' home.

Marcy frowned. "What do you mean?"

"Your mother is going to kill him for thwarting her plans to learn all she could about me." He chuckled, and she laughed softly.

"Oh, no, she won't. She'll pretend to be upset with him, and he'll pretend to be sorry and they'll both end up in each other's arms before two minutes have passed," she predicted with a smile.

"They love each other very much."

"Mmm-hmm, they always have." She sighed enviously. That was what she wanted—with him.

"They remind me of my parents." He glanced at her

long enough to see her nod in agreement. "You were very quiet tonight."

"Complaining?" She smiled, glancing at his profile.

"No. Yes." He shook his head in bafflement. "It's just not like you to be so...subdued."

"I was observing," she confessed.

"Observing what?" He frowned, and she repressed an urge to smooth her fingers over his brow.

"The way you and my parents interacted," she frankly admitted.

"Did you like what you saw?"

"Very much," she replied. "It's important to me that my parents like the man I choose."

"And you think I'm that man?"

"You are." She positively shook her head.

"What if that's not what I want?" he carefully asked.

"It is." Her confident statement elicited a slight smile from him. "You're just reluctant to admit it."

"Why do you think that is?"

"You're a lawyer all right," she said and chuckled. "Partly, I think it's because you don't want to acknowledge how important I am to you and partly because you think your work will come between us somehow," she correctly surmised.

"Why did you say that about my work?" His tone changed from teasing to almost accusatory.

"It's obvious. Your work has kept you away from your family for four years. You're always jetting from one place to another. You're probably afraid I won't be able to handle the demands of your job."

"You think you could?"

"Yes," she simply informed.

He wanted to believe her, but how could he? She had no idea what his job really entailed or how dangerous it was. She'd have to be a saint to put up with the frequent absences, never-ending secrets and the crazy risks he undertook for the sake of a successful mission. He couldn't and wouldn't ask that of her, but if he was free...*if he was free...*

"What are you thinking?"

"Hmm?" He focused on her curious face. "Oh, just that I had a nice time tonight."

"Don't sound so surprised." She laughed.

"I'm not." He nearly groaned as her perfume wafted across him as she pushed her coat off her shoulders. Hell, he wished she would stop moving.

"Yes, you are." She absently brushed her hair behind her ear. That thick, wavy, gorgeous hair he would love to bury his face in.

"Yes, I am," he admitted with a smirk.

"You had a good time even though Mom was giving you the third degree?"

"Even with that," he said, chuckling. "Your father is great."

"And my mother?" A smile played about her lips.

"I like her," he truthfully responded. When he looked at Margaret, he could see how gorgeous Marcy would still be at her age, and he absurdly saw himself beside her at that point in time.

"Really?" She interrupted his disturbing thoughts.

"Yes, I have nothing against your mother. I think she's lovely."

"But?"

"But I wish people would butt out of my personal life," he relented.

"I agree totally."

"You do?" He glanced at her briefly before returning his attention to the road.

"Mmm-hmm." She nodded her head. "It's so frustrating when people think they know what's best for me more so than I do."

"I know what you mean." He shook his head in agreement and didn't see her slight smile as she skillfully led him where she wanted him to go.

"They think we need to be pushed together because that's what they want to see happen," she continued, her dress rustling as she crossed her slender long legs that he would love to run his fingers down the length of. "But what about what we want?"

"Yeah, what about us?" he agreed. Then he added, "Maybe we don't think we're compatible."

"Or maybe we just don't need any outside interference," she countered, sliding her hand toward his leg.

"I thought you were on my side?" He turned suspicious eyes on her briefly.

"I am totally on your side," she whispered. "I don't need any help to capture you, Nathan. I can do it all by myself and I intend to." She then placed a hand on his thigh, causing the car to swerve slightly before he regained control.

"What are you doing?"

"Me?" She squeezed his thigh. "Nothing."

"Marcy, stop touching me." He nearly groaned.

"Why?" She leaned closer as her hand slid higher on his thigh. "Does it bother you?"

"No," he lied.

"No?" She smiled as her fingers lightly outlined the top of his thigh before sliding inward.

"Yes!" He snapped as her hand moved higher ever so close to the painful bulge in his pants.

"As much as I would like to continue this, I'll stop because getting into an accident is not part of my plans for us tonight," she said as she slowly removed her hand.

"What are your plans?" His voice was tight as he fought for control.

"I won't tell you, but I'll show you," she promised with a seductive smile that almost had him stopping the car and crushing his lips to hers.

"I know you will." He managed a tight smile.

"Count on it," she whispered into his ear and softly laughed as his fingers tightened on the wheel.

She slowly moved away from him, and they continued on in electric silence.

"Good night, Marcy." Nathan turned to leave as she stepped inside her condo a short while later.

"Come in for coffee."

"No, I should be going," he declined. She reached out, took his hand and gently pulled him inside.

"I promise I'll keep my hands to myself." She crossed her heart as she switched on a light.

It wasn't *her* hands he was concerned about but rather his own. It was taking all his willpower even now not to grab her, fasten his arms around her alluring body and crush his mouth to hers.

"I don't want any coffee, thank you." He tried to decline gracefully, but she had already steered him over to the sofa.

"Nonsense. We could both use some." She ignored his words. "Have a seat," she offered, walking into the kitchen.

He watched her take off her coat and throw it over a chair. That shimmery blue dress that had been driving him mad all night was uncovered; it revealed very little skin with its long sleeves and high neckline that dipped in the back to reveal the skin of her shoulder blades and midback. There was a huge slit up one side that gave him a wonderful view of silk-clad legs as she walked into the spacious, open kitchen, stopping long enough to kick off her high-heeled shoes. *Oh, Jesus, help me!*

"Sit down," she reiterated, and only then did he realize he was still standing, gawking at her.

He rigidly sat on the sofa but still had a wonderful view of her as she worked preparing coffee. She took out two mugs and a sack from the cabinet.

"Don't go to any trouble for me," he replied as she measured out coffee beans.

"I'm not. I don't use instant coffee." She poured water in the coffeemaker and ground the beans to dust before adding them.

"I see you didn't pick up your mother's lack of culinary skills." He smiled as she moved effortlessly through the kitchen, eyes glancing over the sparkling stainless steel pots and pans that hung over the butcher block center island.

"No, Daddy taught me well." She smiled at him. "I can cook almost anything. I'll cook you dinner soon," she promised and in a few minutes walked back into the living room carrying two black mugs of coffee.

He stood and took one of the mugs from her and then resumed his seat after she sat on the sofa, tucking her feet beneath her.

"You take it black, right?"

"Yes. Nice of you to notice." He purposefully placed some distance between them.

"I notice everything about you Nathan, probably things you aren't even aware of doing," she promised as she sipped her coffee.

"Like what?" He took a drink of his coffee. "This is good."

"Thanks." She moved closer to him so that her thigh

brushed against his. "For example, do you know you rub your chin when you're frustrated?"

"I do not." He frowned at her, and she laughed—soft and sexy.

"Oh, yes, you do. You did it several times tonight when Mom was grilling you," she observed.

He took another sip of his coffee. His eyes furrowed in thought as he tried to digest the validity of her observation.

"What else do I do?"

"You scowl a lot."

"I don't scowl," he contradicted, offended when he realized he was doing it now.

"Yes, you do," she insisted. "But I like it. It makes you look dangerous—and so sexy." She whispered the latter.

He swallowed hard, "Anything else?"

"You try not to touch me, but you always do." Her voice was barely a whisper.

"I'm not touching you now," he challenged. *Though I wish to God I was.* Lord, trying to keep his hands off this woman was killing him.

"Yes you are—with your eyes," she softly contradicted. "They're very expressive. Sometimes when you look at me it's as if I'm transparent."

"Marcy—" He was mesmerized by her voice, her words, simply by her.

"I want to share everything with you."

"You're too honest," he complained, setting his mug down on the table. "One day it's going to expose you too much."

"I don't know any other way to be except honest," she countered. "And I don't mind being exposed to you."

"Maybe you should," he darkly promised.

"I can't hide anything from you, Nathan," she willingly confessed.

He felt both blessed and cursed that she wanted him, and there was no denying he wanted her, but he had promised himself not to get involved while he worked with Black Ops. He had seen his share of team members' relationships destroyed by the enormous subterfuge the job necessitated. He'd vowed to never burden a woman with the demands of his job, but how he wanted to give Marcy a chance to try.

"I rendered you speechless." She smiled.

"No—" he refocused on her beautiful face "—I just…" He paused and asked a question that had been nagging him, "Marcy, what do you see in me?"

"It would take me all night to answer that fully," she said and smiled. "Succinctly, I feel alive when I'm with you. I'm attracted to your soul."

"My soul?" He echoed, intrigued and unnerved.

"Mmm-hmm." She sipped her coffee before continuing. "I don't want to give you a big head here." She laughed and he joined her. "What draws me to you is your kindness, your love of family and your dedication to the people you care about and to your job. You want to make a difference in the world and you do." She continued to smile into his surprised eyes.

"How do you know all that about me?"

"It's there for anyone who knows where to look," she simply stated.

"And you did?"

"I didn't have to look. I just knew it," she whispered. "When we first met, I felt a jolt—something I've never experienced before." She paused trying to find the right words. "Something inside of me just…clicked into place."

"I know," he softly responded. He couldn't have explained his reaction to meeting her any better than she just had.

"Do you?"

"Yes."

"You felt it?"

"I did—I do, and I wish I didn't." he rubbed his chin and slowly stopped as he realized her earlier words had been correct. She tactfully pretended not to notice his actions.

"Why?" She didn't understand why he fought against giving them a chance.

"I'm not someone you should become involved with."

"Too late. I'm already involved with you."

"Marcy—"

"Save your breath, Nathan. I can't change the way I feel any more than you can."

She was right about that. Lord knows he was trying, but he could no more stop wanting or needing her than he could stop breathing.

"Why hasn't some man snapped you up?" he wondered aloud.

"I'm not some piece of meat on a plate to be devoured, Nathan. I won't be snapped up by anyone. But I will give all that I have and am to the man that I choose," she softly ended.

"As it should be."

"As it will be," she promised, making no mistake that he was that man.

"I should be going." Though he said the words, he seemed incapable of acting on them.

"If you must," she whispered, smiling as he continued to stare at her without moving.

She didn't touch him as she had promised, but he, unable to bear any distance between them any longer, pulled her into his arms until she was sitting on his lap. He stared at her for endless seconds, memorizing every curve and line of her gorgeous face, trying to unlock the mystery of her and his feelings for her, and then unable to bear any more distance between them, his lips slid languidly over hers, tasting coffee and the sweet taste that was uniquely her. Her fingers curled around his neck; she sank and was pulled closer as he kissed her deeply, slowly, enjoying every sensation, taste and texture of her. His tongue investigated every crevice of her mouth before engaging in passionate warfare with her own.

Marcy sighed against Nathan's dominant mouth. Every nerve ending in her body stood at attention, and she felt as though she would surely die at any second if he continued to kiss her like this and destruction was even more certain if he dared to stop.

"You're dangerous," he huskily responded, reluctantly releasing her clinging lips.

"No," she disagreed, opening drugged eyes to stare into his equally affected ones. "What you feel for me is dangerous."

"I should go," he reiterated, sliding a hand down her satin-clad hip and back.

"Do you really want to?" Her fingers flexed at his nape.

"No," he groaned, rubbing his lips softly against hers. It wasn't fair that a woman should be this beautiful or fit so perfectly against him—as though that was where she had always belonged and always would be.

"But you're going to," she whispered. Whatever he was looking for, couldn't he see she held it and would give it to him gladly?

"I have to," he painfully decided.

"I could change your mind." Her eyes bore into his, and they both silently acknowledged how true her assertion was.

"I can't let you." He released her and stood.

"Yet," she agreed, also standing.

"Thanks for the coffee." He walked over to the door

and opened it when he really wanted to pull her back into his arms and devour her.

"I'm glad you came to dinner with me." She laced her fingers together so that she wouldn't touch him. He smiled understandingly at her actions.

"Good night." He covered her hands with his briefly and then turned to leave.

"Kiss me again," she softly ordered, stopping him.

He couldn't resist her or his desire. Pulling her into his arms, he did as she asked and as he wanted. His mouth swooped down and captured hers, trying unsuccessfully to feed the gnawing hunger within for the woman in his arms. They kissed for endless, satisfying minutes during which time he silently debated picking her up and carrying her into the bedroom and finishing what he had started. He didn't know how he gathered the strength to command his lips release hers, but they fortunately obeyed him.

"Sleep well," he murmured, reluctantly releasing her.

"I won't without you," she responded.

God, he wished she would stop destroying him with her words, her eyes and her trusting heart.

"Neither will I." He lightly fingered her petal-soft cheek.

"Dream of me," she whispered as he ended contact with her and walked through the door without another word.

As she closed the door and he walked to the elevator, he feared he would have no other choice but to do as she instructed—for the rest of his life.

Nathan slowly awoke in the morning and brushed a hand over his tired eyes. He had spent a restless night having vividly erotic dreams about Marcy. He had gone to bed with her name on his lips and woke up the same way. If he didn't know any better, he would say she had placed a curse on him; she had certainly put him under some sort of spell. No matter what he did or how hard he tried—and he had tried—he couldn't stop thinking about her or wanting her.

The thought of leaving her as he knew he must very, very soon sickened him, but there was no way to avoid the inevitable; if he refused to deploy on a mission he was leading—something he would never do—he'd be arrested, ultimately court-martialed and no doubt receive a hefty prison sentence. He reached out and grabbed his phone from the nightstand, pressing a button to illuminate the face, which revealed it was only 5:32 a.m. He thought about going back to sleep, but what was the use? He wouldn't rest, anyway; he would just keep thinking about and longing for her.

He groaned and made himself get up and prepare for what he instinctively knew would be a long day as he fought the urge to see Marcy. He hesitated glancing toward his phone. His hand levitated to it, but then he angrily snatched it away and instead stalked into the bathroom and switched on the shower. He would not call her, and he certainly wasn't going to see her.

Yeah, good luck with that, he silently ridiculed himself as he stepped under the cold spray of water.

Marcy hummed a bright tune as she laid out her forest-green suit on the bed. Things were progressing very nicely with Nathan—better than she had anticipated. He was coming around; he hadn't wanted to leave her last night—in fact, he had found it extremely difficult to leave her. She had sensed the inner turmoil and wondered why he was convinced it would be better for her if they didn't pursue a romantic relationship. He liked her, he wanted her, but he kept pulling back. Why? She didn't know, but she was definitely going to keep chipping away at his bothersome resolve until it crumbled completely. They were meant to be together; she knew that and so did Nathan, no matter how hard he tried to fight against that inevitability.

She picked up the suit and placed it back in her walk-in closet and took out a red one instead along with a long-sleeved white silk blouse. Nodding in satisfaction, she chose a pair of red pumps and laid them on the bed beside her clothes.

She secured her hair on top of her head with a clip and walked into the bathroom and got into the shower. She wondered how Nathan had slept last night. Had he dreamed of her as she had ordered? If his dreams had been anything like hers, he had awakened with unfulfilled longing and wishing she was lying beside him in his lonely bed.

Picking up the soap, she began lathering herself while contemplating how quickly she could get through her workday so she could see Nathan again.

Chapter 6

Nathan turned as the elevator doors opened revealing the person precipitating his visit to the Johnson Stockbrokerage Firm—Marcy Johnson. She was massaging her temple with one hand while the other carried her coat. Her eyes were closed, and she looked as though she was in pain.

"Marcy, what's wrong?"

"Nathan." She slowly opened exhausted eyes and smiled tiredly. "What a nice surprise."

"Good to see you, Nathan."

"You, too, sir." Nathan shook Michael's hand before returning his attention to Marcy. "Are you okay?"

"I'm fine. Dad and I have just come from the *niecy*."

Nathan's brows furrowed, "Where?"

"The New York Stock Exchange," Michael translated without glancing up from rifling through his messages.

"It was a nightmare. Paper flying, deafening noise and

normally sane people screaming and acting like uncivilized animals!" She groaned at the memory.

"Why do you go there if it gets you upset like this?"

"Upset? I love it." She chuckled before wincing as her head throbbed. She needed to get to her office and her aspirin bottle quickly.

"Oh, sweetie, your mother's coming by tonight with a suit you ordered or something like that," Michael absently shot over his shoulder before entering his office.

"Do I have any messages, Peggy?" Marcy's voice was barely above a whisper.

"Yes, ma'am. Here you go." She handed her several pink slips, which Marcy ignored, closing her eyes and massaging her throbbing temple praying for relief.

"Headache." Nathan touched her shoulder sympathetically.

"Monster." She groaned, partially opening pained eyes to stare into his concerned ones. "Will you carry me into my office?" she joked, motioning to the open door on the left, and nearly leaped with delight as he obligingly scooped her up in his arms.

Peggy sighed enviously as they passed by her.

"You'll have to let go so I can put you down," Nathan instructed seconds later when he stopped behind her glass desk.

"What if I don't want to be put down?" She twined her arms tighter about his neck, bringing her face closer to his.

"Was this an elaborate scheme to get me alone in your office?" He grinned at her.

She smiled impishly. "No, but now that you've planted the seed…"

"Release me, Marcy Johnson," he softly ordered, setting her down in her chair.

She grudgingly did as he instructed but was delighted

when he remained bent over her, lips mere inches from hers. Darkening eyes held hers as he began purposefully unbuttoning her red jacket.

"Why Mr. Carter, what do you have in mind?"

He jealously watched as she ran her tongue over the top of her red painted lips. Her mischievous chuckle informed him she was fully aware of the sexiness of her actions.

"Not too tired to tease me, I see." He lifted her up and pulled the jacket from her, revealing a long-sleeved white silk shirt underneath.

"Never." She frowned and pointed to her desk. "Will you hand me the bottle of aspirin in the top drawer behind you?"

"You don't need aspirin. I have the perfect headache cure."

"What's that?"

"You'll see." He smiled, and swiveling her chair around, he began massaging her neck and shoulders.

"Mmm." She groaned, closing her eyes. "Oh, that feels wonderful!"

"Your headache will be gone before you know it," he promised, fingers continuing to work their magic.

"Not that I'm complaining, but what brings you here today?"

"I was in the neighborhood and thought I'd come see where you work," he lied, running his fingers up and down the back of her neck. The simple, frightening truth was he had been unable to stay away from her.

"Uh-huh." Her voice informed him she wasn't buying his explanation. She sighed when his hand caressed her hair before placing it over one shoulder.

"No disparaging remarks or I'll stop," he threatened, fingers retreating from her neck.

"No, please don't." Her soft plea turned to a moan as

his fingers resumed their magic. "How do you like my office?" Her arm made a limp circle.

"Very nice."

He surveyed the elegant, purely female office as his fingers continued to knead into her flesh. That perfume of hers wafted up to his nostrils, and before he could help himself, his mouth had replaced his hands at the base of her neck.

"Mmm, that feels even better," she approved, raising a hand behind her to cup his slightly stubbly jaw, running a nail down its length.

"How's your headache?"

"What headache?" He chuckled against her neck, sending goose bumps up her arms.

After imbibing her scent, he lifted his head from her flesh and swiveled the chair around until she was facing him and their lips were centimeters apart. She opened tired yet aroused eyes to stare into the darkening depths of his. Before she could speak and before he could think, his mouth captured hers. She closed her eyes again and placed her arms around his neck as he kissed her silly.

His warm, firm mouth took its time feasting on hers. His teeth nibbled at her lips before his tongue took over. Marcy would have fainted had she not been sitting down. When his seeking tongue slid past her teeth to investigate every hidden corner of her mouth before sparring with hers, she moaned invitingly, and the hands behind his head held him closer. His hands moved to her upper thighs, sliding under the short skirt to rub her silk-clad skin maddeningly before slowly moving back down and eventually away from her tingling flesh.

"Don't stop." She sighed as his mouth released hers.

"Stop trying to seduce me." He straightened and removed her arms from around his neck.

"You kissed me," she softly reminded and tiredly leaned back against her chair still holding one of his hands.

"I couldn't help myself," he confessed, staring deeply into her eyes.

"That's music to my ears." She smiled and then raised a hand to her mouth to hide a yawn. "Excuse me."

"How many more hours are you putting in today?" He said anything to take his mind off her delicious mouth.

"Why?" She ran her free hand up his corrugated stomach to rest on his chest. "Do you have plans for me?"

"Marcy…" He paused, lowering his lips back to hers, hovering there, just out of reach.

"Yes?" She sighed, fingers crumpling his shirt front.

"Get some rest tonight," he softly ordered, disentangling his hand from hers, prying her fingers from his shirt and walking away while he still could.

"Don't you want to see me tonight?" she asked through another yawn.

"I don't think you could stay awake to enjoy it," he predicted.

"Try me," she softly countered.

He groaned inwardly when she crossed those shapely legs of hers and seductively stretched, arching her back in precise angles that had her breasts straining against the front of her thin blouse. It was all he could do not to retrace his steps and pull her soft, yielding body into his arms.

"Some other time," he promised, placing his hand on the doorknob.

"Thanks for the lift," she said, smiling as he opened the door. "And especially for the massage."

"Any time," he promised and then left while he still could.

She stared at the door, and a smile lit up her countenance. He had wanted to see her; he had *finally* made the first move. That was very promising—very promising indeed.

That evening, Marcy was securing her hair in a ponytail on the top of her head when the doorbell rang. She walked over barefoot, looked out of the peephole as her mouth burst into a bright smile and quickly opened the door.

Nathan's eyes drifted slowly over her. She was dressed casually in faded jeans and a white midriff sweater—a complete contradiction to the professional attire she had worn earlier. It didn't matter what she wore; she always looked stunning and sexy. Right now, he added *cute* to the list of adjectives.

"Nathan, what a nice surprise." She stepped aside to let him in.

"I guessed you wouldn't feel like cooking." He motioned to the white boxes in his hands.

Her eyes sparkled. "You brought me Chinese?"

"Yeah, do you like it?" He fought an urge to throw the boxes to the floor and fill his arms with her instead.

"I love Chinese, especially Peking duck." She took a box from him and sniffed appreciatively.

"You're in luck, then." He waved another box in front of her.

"Gimme." She grabbed it and plopped down cross-legged onto the carpet, leaning her back against the sofa.

"Do you want to eat there?" He smiled down at her.

"Why not?" she patted a spot beside her, and with a chuckle, he took off his leather jacket, placed it over a chair and sat down beside her as she opened up boxes and placed them on the table in front of them.

"I got a little bit of everything, so I hope you're hungry."

"I'm starved." To prove her point, she plopped some Peking duck into her mouth and chewed appreciatively before swallowing. "This is so sweet of you. Thank you."

"You're welcome, but I told you before that I am not sweet." He balked at her use of the term to describe him.

"Yes, you are." She placed chopsticks holding duck into his mouth.

"Hey, I can feed myself," he protested around a laugh after swallowing.

"But it's more fun this way." She offered him another piece of duck, which he accepted.

She continued feeding him from her carton, and he fed her pepper steak. It didn't occur to either of them to simply pour a little of each onto separate plates; if it did, they quickly dismissed it. There was something intensely appealing and erotic about feeding each other.

"So, are you fully recovered from the NYSE?"

"Yes." She smiled. "Thanks to a handsome gentleman with extremely talented fingers."

"Is that right?" He laughed.

Oh, that was a sound she could definitely get used to. He was always handsome, but when he smiled, he was absolutely gorgeous. Everything about him made her knees go weak and her heart flutter uncontrollably.

"Mmm-hmm." She offered a piece of duck, which he took, and unable to help herself, she placed a light kiss on his lips. He continued to smile at her, but his eyes darkened at her actions. "Thanks."

"For what?" His eyes focused on her tempting, soft lips, which he suddenly wanted much more than food.

"My massage earlier today and for bringing me dinner tonight," she softly explained.

His eyes met hers again, and her smile made it clear she

knew what he had been thinking. It was unnerving and exciting the way she could read him.

"You're welcome."

"Where are the fortune cookies?" she unexpectedly asked, rifling through a brown paper bag until she found them.

"We haven't finished eating yet," he complained, marveling at how quickly she could change directions, always keeping him off balance.

"After we read our fortunes," she argued. "Here, open yours." She handed him one of the brown cookies and waited expectantly for him to read it.

"Confucius say…" His light, teasing voice trailed off as he silently read his fortune. Before he could crumple it up, she took the small white paper from his hands.

"'It is a wise man who realizes when that which he has searched long and diligently for is right before his eyes.'" She read his fortune and lifted smiling eyes to his uneasy ones.

"These things are silly." He discounted the validity of the statement she had just read.

"Oh, I don't know," she contradicted and cracked hers open. "You are going to make love with a tall, secretive, handsome man tonight—and by the way—" she paused and smiled brightly "—his name is Nathan."

"It doesn't say that!" He grabbed at the paper in her hand, which she balled up and tossed onto the table.

"It might as well, because that's what I'm going to do," she whispered, leaning closer to him.

"You really shouldn't…" He stopped as her fingers curled into his shoulders, and she brushed her mouth against his.

"You really should stop fighting the inevitable," she wisely countered.

Their lips touched again tentatively as if they were both afraid of what they didn't know. Then one of them or both of them groaned, and their mouths melted together, tongues meeting and dancing as their long-denied passion erupted. She felt herself being lowered to the floor, and then Nathan's hard body half covered hers. A kiss that had begun so timidly was now bold and aggressive. Mouths pillaged and plundered, and neither of them could stop the destruction their passion unleashed. After a few long minutes, Nathan somehow found the will to pull back, closed his eyes momentarily and silently prayed for strength.

"If you leave me this time, I will kill you," Marcy softly yet seriously whispered as she opened drugged eyes to stare into his conflicted ones.

He knew he should get out of her apartment quickly, but God help him, he didn't know if he possessed the strength to do so. Where was his training? Why was he so utterly helpless when it came to the incomparable woman in his arms? He didn't want to hurt her but feared he was on an unavoidable collision course to do just that.

"Marcy, you don't want to get involved with me." He tried to resist both her and the consuming desire ricocheting through him.

"Yes, I do. I want you very much," she whispered before kissing him again. "And you want me," she softly, yet firmly asserted. "Stop fighting it."

Not even a saint could withstand the temptation Marcy Johnson presented—and he was by no means a saint. He was tired of fighting her and himself. This was wrong; he was going to end up hurting her and he knew it, but he didn't have the strength to walk away from her again. He'd regret giving into their mutual desire in the morning, but he was going to enjoy himself tonight.

"I'm not going to leave you this time," he suddenly

promised against her lips before his mouth covered hers again.

Impatient fingers pulled the band from her hair before entangling in her thick tresses as his mouth continued to pillage. Then his hands slid down her body until they found their way underneath her sweater where to his delight he realized she wasn't wearing a bra. His thumbs rubbed softly and then with increasing urgency across her nipples until they were hard little nubs, and then he cupped her breasts, which fit his hands perfectly. She groaned against his mouth, and her body arched up against his unbending hardness.

His mouth was torn between continuing its dance with hers and tasting the rest of her delectable flesh. Her mouth won for long lingering seconds before he pried his lips away from hers to feast on her softly scented neck—his tongue teasing the pulse beating rapidly there. He inhaled deeply her wonderful scent that fueled the flames of passion coiling within and opened his mouth wide over the base of her neck, teeth gently nibbling and scraping against her soft flesh before his mouth latched on and sucked furiously.

Marcy bit her lower lip to hold back a pleasurable scream. Her hands pulled his sweater up over the waistband of his jeans and explored his muscled back as his hands inched her sweater up while his mouth moved down and greedily engulfed a breast, finally. Oh, what he was doing to her felt wonderful and so right; she moaned loudly then— music to his ears—and his hot mouth opened wider over her softly scented delectable swell. When his teeth took the hard nubbin between them, her back arched off the floor, and her hands dug into his back holding him closer. His hands slid down her flat, quivering stomach, resting just under the waistband of her jeans, fingers deliberately releasing the snap before burrowing beneath the material to caress her lower stomach.

Marcy heard bells vaguely in the distance. Were they in her head? In her heart? As Nathan's hungry mouth, teeth and tongue continued to feast on her breasts, the ringing gave way to an urgent voice calling her name; it took her several seconds to realize it was her mother's voice!

"Marcy, are you in there?" Margaret Johnson yelled through the door.

"Oh, God," Marcy groaned as she fought her way out of a passion-induced stupor.

"Marcy?" Her mother's voice sounded again.

"Nathan?" Hands anchored on the side of his head up, forcing his mouth away from her flesh with difficulty. His body moved up and over hers, and he captured her lips instead. "Nathan, my mother is here," she whispered against his mouth as his body moved seductively against hers. He ignored her words and kissed her again. "Nathan, baby, my mother is here," she replied more urgently, evading his lips with difficulty.

"What?" he thickly asked, biting into her neck, scraping his teeth down her shoulder as his fingers pulled her sweater down her arms.

"Marcy!" Her mother was yelling and rattling her doorknob, bringing her back to reality as a wave of heat swamped her at Nathan's ardent caresses.

"I'm coming, Mom!" Marcy yelled and fought down a hysterical chuckle as she realized how appropriate those words were. Nathan lifted his head to stare at her with passion-glazed eyes.

"Who is that?" he asked, annoyed. She smiled at his disconcertion.

"My mother," she whispered again, pushing at his shoulders and scrambling from beneath him.

"Your mother?" he echoed as he, too, slowly stood. "Oh, hell!"

"I know," she sympathized as she refastened the snap of her jeans.

"Marcy Johnson, if you don't open this door—"

"I'll be right there, Mom!" She kissed his lips softly before walking over to the door. She smoothed a hand over her hair and her thoroughly kissed lips and tried to comb her hair into some semblance of order before opening the door.

"What on earth took you so long to…?" Her mother's voice trailed off, and the irritation that had furrowed her brow disappeared as she noticed her daughter's flushed face before spying Nathan standing by the sofa trying to discretely rebutton his jeans. Margaret didn't need to finish her question; their disheveled appearances bore witness to what she had interrupted. *Hallelujah!*

Nathan felt a huge knot of unfulfilled desire coil in his stomach and was certain Marcy's mother could see that, too, along with the undeniable painful bulge in his pants. How had he allowed things to get so out of control so fast? Logically, he knew it was for the best that Margaret had interrupted them, but a huge part of him wished she hadn't because wrong as it was he wanted nothing more at this moment than to be nestled deep within the woman who had captivated him since their first meeting.

"Mom, what are you doing here?" Marcy adored her mother, but she had never been less happy to see anyone in her life.

"Didn't your father tell you I was bringing this suit you ordered by tonight?" Her mother handed her the garment bag in her hands.

"Um, yes, I think he mentioned it." Marcy took the

bag and carelessly tossed it over a nearby chair. "I—" she glanced briefly at Nathan "—guess I forgot."

"Understandable, dear." Margaret glanced knowingly from one to the other. She couldn't wait to call Linda. "Hello, Nathan." She beamed at him.

"Mrs. Johnson, it's nice to see you again," he lied. He liked her, but he didn't like her at this moment, though he realized he should be grateful to her for stopping them both from making a terrible mistake.

"Have I interrupted anything?"

"No, not at all," Nathan coolly responded and Marcy envied his control. "I was just leaving." He walked over and picked up his jacket.

"Leaving?" Marcy almost wailed as she walked after him. "Excuse me, Mom. I'll be right back," she yelled as she hurriedly followed Nathan out of the apartment and grabbed his arm. "Nathan, don't go."

"Marcy I have to," he said, frustratedly scratching his chin.

"I'll get rid of Mom quickly," she promised.

"Don't be ridiculous. What are you going to do, tell your mother to go home because we want to make love?" His tone conveyed how absurd he thought that would be.

"Why not?" she seriously asked, squeezing his rigid arms.

He wished she wouldn't touch him because it made it impossible for him to think logically. He was hanging on to his sanity by a very slim thread as it was, and it was all he could do not to pull her back into his arms and let madness have its way.

"You would, wouldn't you?" Despite the ache in his loins and his heart, he managed a lopsided grin.

"After all the hard work it took to get you to this point? Damn right I would," she fiercely agreed.

"You said you believed in fate," he reminded while continuously punching the button to summon the infernal elevator, praying it would come quickly.

"I do." She covered his hand with hers and lowered it from the control panel.

"Then maybe your mom stopped us for a reason—because we're not meant to be," he logically concluded.

"I don't believe that." She negatively shook her head.

"Well, I do," he countered, removing his hand from hers as he turned his back on her, hoping she would go back inside, which of course, she didn't.

"No, you don't," she spoke to his back. "You're just looking for an excuse to walk away from me again." Anger began to simmer within her.

"Go back in to your mother."

"So you don't want me?" Tired of talking to his back, she stepped in front of him. "Is that it?"

"No, I don't," he lied through his teeth. He wanted her as he had never wanted anything else in his entire life. "Chalk up my behavior to temporary insanity."

She didn't say a word but instead moved closer until her body was plastered against his. She smiled into his aroused eyes, reached up and pulled his mouth down to hers.

He promised himself he wasn't going to respond to her kiss. That resolve lasted for all of a second. She felt and tasted wonderful—sweet and spicy. After all, he was a red-blooded healthy man, so how the hell was he supposed to stop himself from kissing her back? One of his hands roamed under her sweater spreading across her satiny bare back; the other coiled in her hair, pulling her head back so that his mouth could feast as he took hungry control of the kiss—a kiss that led to another and another. When their mouths parted, his forehead rested against hers; they were both breathing hard, and he was perilously close to taking her in the hallway.

Margaret Johnson slowly closed the apartment door and rubbed her palms together in glee. Things were progressing very well between the children. She would definitely have to call Linda and give her all the juicy details—just as soon as she went on a little fishing expedition with her daughter.

"Liar," Marcy whispered before slowly moving out of his arms and walking back to her door. "We're not finished with this, Nathan," she promised and sauntered back into her apartment.

No, he feared they weren't. This situation was intolerable, but he had only himself to blame. He knew better than this; he should never have touched her, yet common sense seemed to fly straight out of the window whenever he got near Marcy. The elevator finally arrived, and he entered it with a loud sigh. His body ached with need, his blood boiled with unfulfilled desire and he felt like breaking something!

He would feel better once he went home and took a long, freezing shower—a necessary nightly ritual he had become quite accustomed to since meeting Marcy Johnson.

"I'm sorry, dear," Margaret apologized as Marcy returned to her apartment, frustration evident.

"Oh, Mom. I almost had him this time," she wailed in disappointment.

"Marcy Johnson, watch your mouth." Margaret feigned indignation.

"You and Mrs. Carter are the ones trying to get us married off. We're just doing our parts, trying to find out if we're compatible…"

"I didn't raise you to talk like that, young lady," her mother chided as she walked over and smoothed her tousled hair away from her mischievous face.

"Yes, you did." Marcy kissed her cheek before walking away. "We were so close this time." Then she sighed.

"Nathan is special to you," Margaret unnecessarily stated.

"Yes, very special," Marcy softly agreed, turning to face her again.

"And how does he feel about you?"

"He's fighting me—us." Marcy shook her head as she sat heavily down on the sofa.

"What man doesn't?" Margaret's dry tone had her daughter laughing. "How they cling to their infernal freedom like a badge of honor." Margaret shook her head disdainfully.

"Truer words…" Marcy nodded in agreement.

"Don't fret, darling. You'll get another chance, and I promise not to interrupt when that time comes and to flay the skin off of anyone else who tries to," Margaret vowed as she sat down beside her.

"I love you, Mommy." Marcy hugged her tightly.

"I love you, too, baby," Margaret whispered as Marcy snuggled close. "I am sorry I spoiled your plans tonight. If I had known Nathan was here—"

"It's okay. Like you said, we'll have another opportunity and soon," she vowed, a determined glint in her eyes.

"That's my daughter," Margaret approved, kissing the top of her head and squeezing her tightly as she rocked her in her arms, making her laugh.

"Yes, I am," Marcy agreed, squeezing her back.

You got a reprieve tonight, Nathan, but the next time we meet—watch out, Marcy silently promised.

Chapter 7

"Hello."

"Hi, handsome."

"Marcy." Nathan groaned inwardly at the happiness that sprung to life within him at hearing her voice.

"You don't sound glad to hear from me."

"I am." Nathan silently cursed his truthful tongue.

"No denial. That's very good." She laughed at his audible sigh. "What are you doing today?"

Trying to stay away from you—a task that's harder than anything I've ever undertaken. It had been two days since their passionate encounter in her apartment during which time he had somehow refrained from calling her. Frankly, he hadn't known how much longer he could hold out. He should have known she would make a move since he hadn't.

"I have some work I need to get done," he finally answered.

"You're on vacation, Nathan, and besides, it's Saturday—time to relax."

"I don't do relaxation well."

"You should know better than to challenge me."

"That wasn't a challenge," he said and smiled. "It was a statement of fact."

"Well, I took it as a challenge, and as such, I have to prove you wrong."

He laughed in spite of himself. "How do you plan to do that?"

"By taking you to the Bronx Zoo."

He paused before repeating, "The zoo?"

"Yes." She laughed. "You know the place where they house all types of animals."

He chuckled. "Yes, I know what a zoo is."

"Will you come with me?"

Nathan opened his mouth to tell her he couldn't make it, but instead he asked, "What time?"

"Around noon. Is that good for you?"

"That's fine."

"Great, I'll see you then." She paused before saying, "And Nathan?"

"Yes."

"Prepare to relax and have fun." With that, she rang off.

As he hung up his phone, he couldn't help laughing out loud. If his team members could see him now, they wouldn't recognize him; he barely recognized himself since meeting Marcy. Where was the no-nonsense, determined soldier who wisely shied away from personal relationships and recommended his men do the same while they were involved in Black Ops? He was a first-rate hypocrite for engaging in the very behavior he had warned them about more times than he could count.

He should call Marcy back and cancel; yep, that's what

he *should* do, but he knew he wouldn't because the simple truth was he couldn't wait to see her again.

Two hours later, Marcy and Nathan were at the zoo—on a date. Both were similarly dressed in faded jeans, light sweaters and leather jackets. They walked around for hours glancing at animals, holding hands, having ice cream and cotton candy and riding the train.

He was having a wonderful time—something that came very easily to him whenever he was around Marcy. She was so easy to be with—so impossible to stay away from.

"You love animals, don't you?" He smiled as they leaned against a rail watching a pair of giraffes, their graceful, long necks reaching to strip leaves from the trees that compromised one side of their habitat.

"Very much." She turned to smile at him. "I would have a big house full of them if I could," she admitted, fighting a groan as he brushed a stray strand of hair out of her eyes. His fingers continued to slide absently through her long tresses; she doubted he was even aware he was doing it.

"Why don't you have any pets?" He removed his fingers from her hair and grabbed her hand as they strolled away.

"I'd love some dogs, but I spend so much time at work. Besides, I'd have to get a house with a big yard so that they could run free." She laced her fingers with his, and he unconsciously pulled her closer to his side.

They stopped walking to watch a pack of Asian elephants slowly moving around their domain, trunks swinging from side to side as they sauntered.

"They're marvelous, aren't they?" She enthused as she watched them.

"I saw some when I was in Asia and Africa last year," he stated matter-of-factly.

"You really do travel all over the world, don't you?"

She turned questioning eyes on him. "Isn't that odd for a lawyer?"

"Not when you work for the State Department. We have clients worldwide," he smoothly replied.

"I guess you would," she agreed as he pulled her away. "I tried to get tickets for a sleepover, but they were all sold out."

"A what?" He stopped and stared at her perplexed.

"A sleepover." She laughed. "Didn't you ever stay at one when you were a child?" At his negative nod, she explained, "A sleepover is an event the zoo puts on where they allow people to spend the night and wake up with the animals."

He decided it was a good thing they had been sold out. The last thing he needed was to sleep beside her all night and be expected to behave like a gentleman.

"Maybe some other time."

"For the sleepover at the zoo or just with me," she teased as they walked on.

"Marcy…" He stopped and shook his head; he didn't know what to say to her.

"Oh, I know. I'm a handful." She chuckled.

"More like an armful," he corrected, taking her hand again as they walked on.

"But you've got very strong, capable arms, Nathan," she whispered. Though he remained silent, the heated look he gave her spoke volumes. "How about a late lunch?"

"You can't be hungry." He was aghast. They had eaten nothing but junk for the three hours they had been there.

"Not really," she admitted. "I just don't want the day to end."

"Neither do I," he easily confessed, and she stopped to happily stare at him.

"No?"

"No," he echoed.

"Well, in that case, I know this place that serves the best food, and they even have entertainment," she promised as they walked off.

"Is that a fact?" He smiled and entwined his fingers with hers as he pulled her closer to his side.

"Yeah," she breathed.

"That sounds interesting." He bobbed his eyebrows. "What kind of entertainment?"

"You'll see," she mysteriously promised.

"What are we waiting for, then?"

"Follow me," she softly ordered, and they left hand in hand.

They had just exited the zoo and taken only a few steps when two young men purposefully blocked their way. Nathan quickly sized up the situation and knew the pair was up to no good—a fact that was confirmed when one of the men spoke.

"Hey, baby, wanna date a real man?"

Marcy swept contemptuous eyes over him and his friend. "I'm with the only real man in the immediate vicinity."

The man jeered, "You've got a smart mouth on you, baby."

"I'm not your baby," Marcy icily replied.

"We could change that." The man reached out a hand to touch her, which Nathan quickly intercepted.

"Don't touch her!" Nathan's hard eyes, steely voice and fighting stance promised he was ready to back up his order with action.

"What you gonna do about it, pretty boy?" The man opened his jacket, revealing a gun.

Nathan pushed Marcy behind him and threatened, "If you don't get out of our way, you'll find out."

The man took out the gun and pointed it at them. "Make me."

Nathan did the last thing any of them expected—he laughed. The men glanced at each other uneasily but refused to back down.

"You should put that away before you hurt yourself," Nathan suggested.

"Give me your wallet." The gunman turned his attention to Marcy, "And your purse, sweet thing."

"Don't even think about it." Nathan pushed Marcy farther behind him when the second man pulled out a switchblade.

"You're just begging for a beat down, dumbass."

"You took the words right out of my mouth." Nathan smiled menacingly and with lightning-fast reflexes punched each one, disarming the punk of his gun and the other of his knife before sending them crashing to the ground before Marcy could even blink. She couldn't believe her eyes when she saw the two would-be robbers sprawled across the concrete, moaning and holding various parts of their bodies. Her mouth dropped open in shock as her wide eyes refocused on Nathan, who didn't have a scratch on him.

A small crowd quickly gathered, and zoo security appeared out of nowhere and took charge of the situation. Nathan gave them the gun and knife and said a few words to them before returning to Marcy's side.

"Are you okay?"

"I'm fine." Marcy glanced at him in awe. "Did the marines teach you to fight like that?"

"They did, but mostly it was growing up in New York." He grabbed her hand and laughed, pulling her away from the gathering crowd.

* * *

A short while later, Marcy and Nathan sat in the Park Avenue Country Club Sports Bar. They occupied a small round table almost directly in front of a huge television set, which comprised almost an entire wall. They ate hot wings and potato wedges and drank draft beer. An uptown woman like Marcy Johnson should have seemed very out place here, but she didn't. She wasn't a stranger, either, a fact he became aware of the moment they walked in from the various greetings she received.

"What?" Nathan asked at Marcy's amazed stare.

"You're like James Bond."

He laughed. "Thanks for the compliment, but I don't think he has anything to worry about from me."

"That's not true," she disagreed. "You're a lethal weapon."

His smile widened. "I just know how to take care of myself."

"That's an understatement if ever I heard one. You disarmed two armed thugs, knocked them out in seconds and they didn't even land one blow on you."

"Are you complaining?"

"No, it's just…" She paused before sighing. "Wow!"

"Marcy—"

"Hey, Marcy, care for a friendly wager on the game," A man stopped by their table and nodded to Nathan. "Hi, I'm Joe," he said as he extended his hand.

"Joe, this is Nathan." Marcy did the introductions as the two shook hands.

"Nice to meet you." Nathan smiled, grateful for Joe's timely intervention.

"So what about it, gorgeous? Wanna bet with me?" Joe smiled at Marcy. Even though the man was in his fifties, Nathan noted the sparkle in his eyes as he glanced at the beauty beside him. "I'll bet you the Los Angeles' wipes the floor with your guys."

"Sure, Joe, how much you want to lose?" She smiled up at him sweetly.

"How about twenty?" The man took out a bill and placed it on the table. Marcy dug into her purse and did the same.

"You're on," she promised, adding smugly, "You can just leave that here since it'll be mine soon."

"We'll see." Joe laughed and walked off.

"Hey, Sam, how about another draft?" Marcy yelled over the noise, and the bartender nodded at her. Seconds later, a waitress had replaced their empty glasses with full ones.

"How often do you come here?" Nathan asked as he took a drink of his beer.

"At least once a week. I enjoy watching basketball here."

"What game?" He laughed when his innocent question caused her to nearly choke on her drink.

"What game?" She gasped, appalled. "New York—basketball."

"Oh." He shook his head.

She popped a few peanuts into her mouth. "Do you enjoy basketball?"

"I never have much time to watch. I try to catch football when I can." He smiled as she continued eating peanuts. How much junk could her system hold in a day?

"Well, you're in for a treat tonight," she promised, switching to pretzels. "Los Angeles is playing New York."

"Sounds exciting," he absently replied. He couldn't imagine anything being as exciting as just staring at her was.

"It will be once the game starts and this place starts

hopping." She glanced at her watch. "Which should be in a few minutes."

"So this is how you relax after a hard day at work?"

"Sometimes," she agreed. "Sometimes I like to go home, let my hair down, put on something really comfortable and…" She deliberately lowered her voice before allowing it to taper off.

He sat forward expectantly. "And what?"

"I think I'll show you in person," she promised, smiling. "Soon."

"You enjoy teasing me, don't you?" He trailed a finger across the back of her hand, sending delicious shivers up her arm.

"Mmm," she agreed. "I told you I like to play," she reminded him.

"And I told you I don't." He turned her hand over so that his fingers could glide up her palm to her wrist.

"Didn't," she breathlessly corrected.

He frowned at her, "What do you mean *didn't?*"

"We played all day, and you enjoyed it," she said as she smiled smugly.

"Maybe I did." His eyes never left hers as his fingers traced down her palm to her fingertips before ending contact.

"You did, and I promise you we're not through playing yet," she softly vowed.

Thankfully before he could respond, the game started, and her attention was glued to the television. He soon realized she wasn't just trying to impress him; she was really into the game. He spent more time watching her than the game. As with everything else, she put everything she had into participating in the game, and she did participate, not just watch.

"Come on! Shoot a three, a three!" she yelled, and the

player seemed to hear her because he did just what she had been loudly clamoring for. "Did you see that?" She turned excited eyes on him. "What a shot!"

"Just luck," Joe dismissed her from a few tables down.

"You won't even miss this." She held up both their twenties and laughed at his good-natured scowl. When she returned her eyes to Nathan, he was looking at her as though he had never seen her before. "What?"

"Nothing…nothing," he denied as she laughed knowingly.

"What is it, Nathan? Surprised that a woman can actually enjoy and know something about sports?"

"Not at all," he quickly denied. "It's just that you get so into it." He tried to explain the strange feelings that had ripped through him as he had watched her today and tonight.

"There's no use in doing anything without any emotion," she said and then took a sip of her beer. "Don't you agree?"

"I guess." He bit into a hot wing so he wouldn't have to talk anymore, and she turned twinkling eyes back toward the television.

An hour into the game, he came to the astonishing realization that he wasn't the least bit tired of being with her; he was having a wonderful time. He had been with her all day and longed to spend what hours remained with her. When he had agreed to their date today, he had hoped being in her presence for hours on end would grate on his nerves and that he would be counting the seconds until they parted ways; however, the opposite had happened.

She was smart, funny and easy to be with; she made him relax as he never had before, and he liked her. He knew he wanted her; there was no use denying that, but dammit, he really *liked* her. More than that, he was beginning to care about her—a lot.

That was another reason for him to cut her loose fast—he didn't want to hurt her. However, if he continued seeing her and let things get serious between them—more serious than they already were—he knew without a doubt he was going to do worse than hurt her. He would end up destroying her, and that was something he refused to do.

His life was nothing but lies, subterfuge and secrets. Marcy deserved better than that. She wanted and needed a home and family—someone who would be here for her, not traipsing all over the world at a moment's notice barging headfirst into unimaginable danger. He couldn't give her the simple life she seemed to crave—a life he also craved because of her but knew he couldn't have because his life revolved around perfectly ordered chaos and unimaginable danger. He had to find the strength once and for all to leave her alone.

Marcy turned to say something, and her smile froze at Nathan's somber, almost pained, expression.

"What's wrong, Nathan?" She covered his hand with hers.

"Nothing," he coolly replied, removing his hand from contact with her. "Are you ready to go?"

She wasn't, but it was clear he was. What was the matter with him?

"Now? The game's not over," she reminded him.

"I know, but I'm ready to leave." He stood. "Are you coming?"

"I guess so," she slowly agreed, standing.

"Hey, Marcy, are you leaving?" Joe asked in surprise.

"Yeah, Joe. Hang on to this." She smiled as she handed him their bet money. "I'll collect it later."

As they walked out, she noticed Nathan purposefully

didn't touch her—no holding hands as they had done all day, no playing with her hair, no walking close, no putting his arm around her shoulders. He was cold, aloof and completely the opposite of the man she had spent a thoroughly enjoyable day with.

"Nathan?"

"Yeah?" He didn't look at her as they continued to walk, and she grabbed his rigid biceps and yanked him to a stop.

"I won't let you pretend that you didn't enjoy being with me today." She correctly guessed his intentions.

"That's not what I'm trying to do," he denied, removing her fingers from his arm.

"No?" An eyebrow rose, and shoulders squared at his actions.

"No," he coolly reiterated.

"Then what?" she demanded, placing her hands on her hips.

"I was just ready to leave." He continued walking, and she had no choice but to follow suit.

"You were uncomfortable because you realize that in addition to wanting me you also like me. Isn't that the truth?" A hand on his arm halted him again.

"No, I was just ready to go." His irritation resulted from her correct assertion. He was also frustrated—in more ways than one. "Why do you have to take everything so personally?"

"Because it *is* personal between us, Nathan Carter—very personal!" she emphatically informed him. "That's what bothers you, isn't it?" As he remained silent, she pleaded for understanding, "Why Nathan? Why are you so afraid of me—of us?"

"There is no us, Marcy," he coldly informed her.

"There is no us?" she echoed disbelievingly. "After the other night when you all but made love to me on my living room floor with my mother standing outside in the hall, you can stand there and emotionlessly say there is no us?" Her voice fractionally rose.

"I wanted you. I won't deny that, but that's all we have between us, Marcy. Mutual lust." He should be struck by lightning for his blatant lie.

"Well." The single word was painfully whispered.

He could kick himself for being the one to place the undisguised hurt in her beautiful eyes, but it was for the best. *It was for the best.* That didn't stop him from feeling like a first-rate heel. "Marcy…" He reached out a hand in her direction, which she pointedly avoided.

"Why don't you go ahead, hide away in your lonesome little hotel suite and tell yourself some more delusions." Her eyes quickly turned to ice. "I can see myself home."

"Don't be ridiculous. I'll take you home." Again, he extended a hand toward her, which she halted with a frosty stare.

"I don't need to be taken home," she responded through gritted teeth and then walked away before stopping and storming back to glare at him. "You haven't seen the last of me, either," she vindictively promised.

Despite feeling lousy about hurting her, he smiled as he watched her abruptly walk away again; this time, she kept going without looking back.

No, he was certain he hadn't seen the last of Marcy Johnson, and to his relief and dismay, he was glad he had not.

"Nicole, I'm twenty-eight and feel like seventy-eight. Your brother is going to make me gray before my time!" Marcy darkly prophesied as they sat at lunch the next day.

"What has he done?" Nicole listened sympathetically while Marcy described their zoo date the day before.

"He likes me. That's the weird thing," Marcy frustratedly concluded. "But for some reason, he won't allow himself to give into what he feels. It's like he's trying to protect me from…" Her voice trailed thoughtfully off.

"From what?" Nicole questioned.

"I don't know." She shook her head in bafflement. "Himself?"

"That doesn't make any sense." Nicole frowned as she tried to unravel her brother's behavior. "I know he'd never hurt you."

"I know that, too," Marcy said and sighed. "You see my dilemma." At Nicole's nod, she took out her cell phone from her purse. "Maybe I should call him."

"Oh, no, don't do that. Give him a few days to realize he misses you," Nicole suggested. "Let him call you."

Marcy chewed at her lower lip. "You think he will?"

"I know he will. My brother may be many things but a fool isn't one of them." Nicole covered her friend's hand comfortingly.

"Maybe he needs a little prodding."

"Like what?" Nicole's eyes lit up at the look of consternation on her face.

"I don't know, but I'm sure something will come to me." Marcy's chuckle turned into a full-blown laugh as on cue an appealingly wicked idea took shape in her mind.

"Marcy Johnson," she spoke absently into the phone while typing on her laptop.

"Hi, Marcy. It's Nathan."

She didn't need to be told that; she recognized his voice instantly. Her heart somersaulted in her chest, and she smiled at Nicole's correct assertion that he would call her. She was thrilled; however, she deliberately kept her voice cool.

"Yes—" she reclined back in her chair "—what can I do for you?"

He sighed heavily. "Your mother just called and invited me to dinner."

"I thought she would."

"Are you going to be there?"

"Of course."

Her smile widened as he sighed again. She was glad he couldn't see her; it was much easier to pretend disinterest over the phone.

"I was wondering if you'd like to go with me."

"Why?" She studied her manicured nails and stifled a laugh at his long pause, which followed her simple question.

"What do you mean *why?*"

"A few days ago, you made it crystal clear you didn't want to spend any time with me," she pointedly reminded. "So what's changed?"

"I didn't say that, Marcy."

"Didn't you?"

"No." His voice hardened as he said, "And you know it."

"That's the way it sounded to me."

"Marcy—"

"Thanks for the invitation, Nathan, but I have to decline."

"Why?"

She grinned at his disbelieving tone. This was just too delicious, and he deserved every second of angst she was inflicting upon on him!

"Because I don't want to go with you," she coolly responded and hung up the phone before he could respond.

She immediately felt a twinge of regret as she stared at the phone but squared her shoulders in resolve. This was phase one in *operation get Nathan to open up,* and she was determined to stick to her guns.

She was going to teach Nathan a much-needed lesson, and her mother's get-together had created the perfect opportunity for her. Reclining in her chair, a smile of anticipation lit up her face; she couldn't wait until dinner because this was going to be a game-changing night.

Chapter 8

Marcy entered her parents' home dressed to destroy in an emerald-green, figure-hugging, just above-the-knee-length dress that left her shapely long legs and back exposed. Her arms were covered in sheer chiffon full-length sleeves. She wore her hair loose and flowing; it framed her shoulders and face in a multitude of curls—a style she knew would torture Nathan all night. She also brought along one other little gem specially designed to make Nathan's night miserable—Henry Robertson, her date.

All heads turned in her direction when Marcy and Henry entered the living room. Henry's arm possessively rested around Marcy's waist, and she smiled up at him and laughed when he whispered something into her ear. Of course, her parents knew that Henry was just a good friend and business associate, but no one else did—particularly Nathan Carter.

Nathan's eyes narrowed into barely visible slits as he

watched Marcy and her date say hello to his parents before moving farther into the room to speak to hers. He felt as if someone had punched him hard in the gut in a sneak attack, and he didn't like the feeling one little bit. Who the hell was this yuppie Marcy was with, and more importantly, why did seeing her with another man produce blinding rage within him? Of course, he knew the answer to that question but refused to acknowledge it. This was going to be a long and miserable night!

Marcy smiled blindingly as her eyes made contact with Nathans's. Her smile increased his scowl of displeasure at seeing her with another man. *Oh, my, he was very angry. Perfect. Mission partly accomplished.*

"Hello, dear." Margaret's greeting forced her daughter's gaze away from Nathan's.

"Hi, Mom." Marcy kissed her cheek. "I hope you don't mind me bringing Henry along to what was supposed to be a family dinner."

"That depends on what you're up to, my darling daughter." Margaret smiled.

"I'm just making a point," Marcy sweetly answered, eyes dancing with mischievousness. "Nathan needs a wake-up call, and Henry is helping me deliver it to him."

"In that case, I don't mind at all," her mother assured, kissing her cheek before leaving to report to Linda that everything was all right.

"Hi, Marcy." Nicole walked up beside her.

"Hey." Marcy hugged Nicole as she walked over.

"Marcy…?"

"Mmm-hmm?" She felt Nathan's eyes on her and refused to obey their silent command to look at him.

"Who's your date?"

"Henry Robertson."

"A friend?"

"Mmm." Marcy briefly glanced at Nathan, who seemed ready to burst before returning her attention to Nicole's concerned face. "Keep a secret?"

"Of course." Nicole leaned closer.

"He's an old friend and business associate, nothing more," she whispered with her back strategically positioned to Nathan's ever-present glaring eyes.

"Good." Nicole sighed in relief. "I can't see you with anyone else except my brother."

"Neither can I, but..." Her voice trailed off expressively.

"But—" Nicole grinned "—you decided to show him there are other fish in the sea."

"In a matter of speaking." Marcy laughed. The sound drifted toward Nathan and set his teeth on edge.

"Well, it's definitely working." Nicole's eyes sought out her brother's, and she shuddered at the frosty gaze he directed at them. "He's absolutely livid."

"I know," Marcy cooed, amusedly following her gaze.

"You're very cruel." Nicole laughed.

"Hey, I'm just trying to break through your stubborn brother's defenses."

"I think you've found the perfect weapon."

"So do I," Marcy agreed.

"Here you go, beautiful." Henry handed her a drink and placed a possessive hand on her waist. "Hello." He directed a dazzling smile at Nicole.

"Thanks." Marcy took her drink, and for Nathan's benefit, she deliberately kissed Henry's cheek near his mouth. "This is Nicole, my good friend."

"Nice to meet you." Nicole offered her hand and blushed when Henry brought it to his lips before releasing it.

"It's a pleasure." Dancing brown eyes smiled back at her before Nicole excused herself with a wink to Marcy.

"How am I doing?" Henry asked lightly, squeezing Marcy's waist.

"Brilliantly." She beamed at him, moving closer to his side.

"You know, I don't mind helping you out, and Lord knows it's no hardship spending an evening with you."

"But?"

"But that guy across the room looks ready to commit murder, and I am much too young to die," Henry theatrically professed.

"Don't worry. I'll protect you," she promised.

"Who's going to protect you?" Henry wanted to know.

Before she could respond, someone touched her arm. She knew who it was before turning to find an obviously upset Nathan glaring at her.

"I need to speak with you now," Nathan demanded.

"I'm busy." She turned back to Henry, preparing to ignore him.

"Marcy."

She turned around again to stare at him. He didn't say anything else but just her name spoken softly yet urgently, and the intensity of his eyes moved her. After several silent seconds, she turned back to her date.

"Henry, will you excuse me for a minute?"

"Of course." He glanced at Nathan's dark countenance and added, "If you're sure."

"I am." Marcy smiled and kissed his cheek. "You've got a minute," she informed a fuming Nathan, walking off ahead of him.

Nathan glared at Henry before following Marcy to the other side of the room where they were relatively alone— as alone as they could be in a room full of family members whose curious eyes glanced their way frequently. He wished they could go somewhere and talk privately.

"All right, say your piece so I can get back to my date."

"What's going on, Marcy?" Nathan fought to keep his voice low, though it was noticeably tinged with anger.

"I don't know what you're referring to," she coolly denied.

"Then I'll spell it out for you—" he motioned toward Henry "—why did you bring that jerk tonight?"

An eyebrow rose. "Where is it written that I can't have a date?"

"I called and invited you *myself*," he reminded through gritted teeth.

"I didn't want to come with you."

"Why not?"

"Not that I need to give you a reason," she delighted in reminding him, "but to be blunt, because I wanted to spend the evening with someone who enjoys being with me and who doesn't have to be tricked or coerced into spending time in my presence."

His eyes narrowed. "What is that supposed to mean?"

"I'm sure you'll figure it out."

She turned to leave. He grabbed her hand, halting her exit. She glanced down at their locked hands, and then frosty eyes rose to encounter his frustrated ones. At her silent demand, he released her and scratched his chin.

"We're not finished here, Marcy," he tightly promised.

"Oh, yes, we are definitely finished here," she haughtily proclaimed before sauntering away, when she really wanted to stay by his side.

As he watched her go, his blood began to boil to the erupting stage. He took a few determined steps after her but stopped when her mother proclaimed dinner was ready.

He simmered all through the meal and didn't know what he ate. He watched Marcy at the other end of the table sitting close to her date, laughing up at him like an idiot all evening. The bum could barely keep his hands off her. He was vaguely aware that Nicole tried to engage him in conversation, but she gave up after he continued to answer her in monosyllabic words. It took an eternity for the meal to end. Once it did, he wished it never had because Marcy and her date took up residence in the middle of the family room and started to slow dance.

Nathan seethed, as he had done for the past half hour as Marcy and Henry danced much too closely for his taste. He watched jealously as the other man's hand splayed widely across Marcy's bare back and pulled her closer—something he thought was impossible, as they were already plastered together. *Enough was enough!* He downed his drink in one gulp and made his way determinedly toward them. He was going to end this charade of Marcy's now!

"Uh-oh," Henry groaned.

"What?" Marcy frowned up at him.

"That glowering guy is headed our way."

She followed his gaze and saw Nathan stalking toward them. He looked angry enough to commit murder.

"Don't worry." She shrugged dismissively. "His bark is worse than his bite."

"Are you sure? He looks pretty fierce to me."

"Trust me. Everything will be fine," Marcy promised.

"I need to talk to you, Marcy."

Marcy casually glanced at Nathan. "Again?"

"Yes," Nathan hissed. "Again."

"Can't it wait? Henry and I haven't finished our dance."

"Oh, yes, you have." Without another word, Nathan took her hand and guided her away from everyone in the room, not stopping until they occupied a secluded corner by themselves.

"We need to talk privately. Get your things." Her eyebrow rose at his tight order. "I'm taking you home."

"The only person I'm going home with is my *date*," she emphasized. "We have a big night planned."

Her last words hit home as she had intended. Nathan's eyes hardened perceptibly, and his mouth became a thin, angry line.

"I've had enough of your theatrics, Marcy. You're leaving with me," he adamantly informed. "You have a choice—you can walk out of here, or I'm going to carry you out."

"Who do you think you are?" She pulled her hand from his. "I will not be manhandled or ordered around by you."

"You don't seem to mind being pawed by Herman," he quickly shot back.

"His name is Henry."

"I don't care what his name is." His eyes darkened. "He's been nearly undressing you all night!"

Her hands rose to her hips. "He has not!"

"The only reason your dress is still on is because it's plastered to your skin," he insulted.

"How dare you!"

"How dare me?"

"Make up your mind, will you!" Her hands dropped from her hips, balling into fists at her sides. "You can't have your cake and eat it, too!"

"Meaning?"

"Meaning you said you didn't want me and that I meant nothing to you. Well, guess what, I finally got the message and moved on. Now you see me with another man and go ballistic when you have no right to comment on anything I do and certainly not who I choose to spend my time with," she meticulously spelled it out for him.

"I never said any such thing," he quickly denied.

"You implied it, and you know it." She poked him in the chest with her finger.

"Marcy." He grabbed her hand and held it against his chest. "I'm in no mood to play these games with you."

"You are so egotistical!" She tried unsuccessfully to free her hand from his. "I am not playing games, but you are and I'm sick of it."

"Exactly what is it you're sick of?"

"You and your mixed signals," she angrily informed him, still trying to retrieve her hand. "Make up your mind, Nathan. Do you want me or not?"

Each was oblivious to every eye in the room being unshakably glued on them as their argument escalated. As far as they were concerned, only the two of them existed.

Nathan disregarded her question and confidently asserted, "You don't want Herbert."

"His name is Henry. *Henry!*" she corrected and resisted the urge to stomp her foot in outrage. "Now answer my question."

"All right, I'll answer your question," he promised, moving closer so that she could see and feel every angry nuance emanating from him. "Go home with Herbert, and give him a story to boast about to his yuppie friends, I don't give a damn what you do or with whom," he angrily promised.

"Neither do I," she snapped. He dropped her hand, and she pivoted away before she gave into the urge to slap his handsome face; she wouldn't give him that satisfaction.

He watched her walk over and plant a lingering kiss on her date's startled mouth before grabbing his hand and marching from the room with him in tow; she never glanced back in his direction once.

When she left, Nathan ignored everyone, walked straight for the bar and began a downward descent into drunkenness. A few minutes later, Nicole was the only one brave enough to approach him as he downed his third—or was it his fourth?—drink.

"Wow! That was some scene between you and Marcy."

"I don't want to talk about it, Nicole."

"Too bad. We're going to, anyway."

He sighed heavily and poured himself another drink. "Go ahead. Have your say."

She touched his rigid arm and shook him gently, "Nathan, stop being crazy and go to Marcy—unless you really want to see her with another man."

"I don't care who Marcy dates."

"Oh, really." Nicole's eyebrow rose disbelievingly. "Is that why you are trying to drain the Johnsons' liquor supply?"

"I'm just thirsty," he countered, halting the glass halfway to his lips before slamming it back on the bar.

"Nathan—"

"I've had enough for one night," he interrupted her. "I'll talk to you later."

"What are you going to do?"

"Go home," he soberly replied.

"Are you sure that's where you're heading?"

"What do you think? That I'm going to run after Marcy, beat up that jerk she brought here tonight and carry her away somewhere like a Neanderthal?"

"Maybe you should."

"I wouldn't give her the satisfaction," he stubbornly refused. "I'm going home." *To drink myself into a stupor without prying eyes, to try to forget Marcy Johnson exists.*

He hurriedly made his apologies to Marcy's parents and to his and then left. The cab ride back to the hotel was short and miserable. When he returned to his suite, he went straight to the bar, took out a bottle of Courvoisier—that would do to start with.

An hour later, he stood staring broodingly out of the window. Not even the liquor he had consumed at the Johnsons' and since coming home had dulled his ability to think about Marcy.

She was with Herman at this moment. He was touching that petal-soft skin. His lips were exploring her luscious sweet mouth. His body was pressed close to the soft, rounded curves he had indelibly memorized. Was she making those wonderful throaty sounds for Herman? Was she lying naked beneath him now writhing in ecstasy?

Damn her and himself for falling for her! How had she insinuated herself into every part of his being in such a short time? How could his life seem so miserably lonely and meaningless without her in it? He hadn't wanted or intended to get involved with her; he didn't want to care about her—but unfortunately, he did. He wanted and needed Marcy with a singular obsessive passion that was methodically destroying the rigid control he had always maintained over his life—and more importantly his heart.

He placed a palm on the window and leaned his forehead against it, staring into the blackness echoing his inner turmoil. His unexpected feelings for Marcy complicated things immensely. He didn't have much time left before his next mission would take him far away from New York and from her for God knows how long. For that reason, he should be happy that she had brought that jerk to dinner tonight; it gave him an excuse to cut her loose before either of them got in any deeper.

Unfortunately, it was much too late to rein in his growing feelings for Marcy, and he knew it because the single thought raging through his mind torturing him at this moment was the fact that Marcy was now with another man instead of being with him—where she belonged.

* * *

For two days, Nathan missed Marcy terribly—her infectious laughter, her beautiful smile and the special way she alone made him feel. Life was colorless without her—dull, gray and listless. He remained secluded in his hotel room not talking to his family or anyone else while fighting with himself not to call her, but on the third day, he lost the useless internal battle and gave into his heart.

"Marcy Johnson." Cool, professional tones answered the phone. "Hello?" she continued when there was no response.

"Marcy, it's Nathan."

She nearly dropped the phone and was glad he couldn't see her. She had begun to think she had made a terrible mistake declining his dinner invitation and presenting Henry as a potential lover to him several nights ago.

"Yes, is there something I can do for you?"

She should win an Oscar for sounding unmoved yet slightly annoyed when she really felt like shouting in delight. He had called her!

"I'm sorry," he forced himself to admit.

"Sorry? What do you have to be sorry about?" She pretended ignorance and placed a hand over the mouthpiece so he wouldn't hear her chuckle triumphantly.

"For hurting your feelings the other day and for being an ass the other night and embarrassing you in front of our families." He sighed audibly.

"The other night?"

"Come on, Marcy…" His voice held frustration.

"Come on and what?"

She reclined in her chair and stared unseeingly out of her office window. A huge smile lit up her countenance. She wasn't going to give him the tiniest bit of a break—yet.

"Will you forgive me?"

"Well, I don't know."

"Do you want me to grovel?" Resentment echoed in every word.

"You weren't very nice the other night," she unnecessarily reminded.

"I know." When she remained silent, he reiterated, "I'm sorry."

"Are you? Truly?"

"Would plastering the words on a billboard in Times Square convince you?" His voice held more than a hint of annoyance.

"I should make you." She secretly smiled.

"But you won't," he correctly surmised.

She wondered if he was smiling—one of those gorgeous smiles she saw so rarely and loved so much. She ran fingers through her hair as she swiveled in her chair.

"Who says I won't?"

"I do," he affirmed. "I know you."

"Not as well as I'd like you to," she impishly responded, enjoying their war of words.

He chuckled before asking, "Will you have lunch with me?"

"You want to spend some time with me?" She enjoyed needling him. Served him right for the miserable two days and nights she had spent.

"Obviously." He sighed, steeling himself to keep his cool. She was the most frustrating, irritating, gorgeous woman he had ever met, and he wanted her with every breath he took. "Well, will you?"

"Today?" she coolly asked.

"Yes." He almost hissed the word, and she repressed a chuckle behind her hand.

"I have to check my schedule," she matter-of-factly answered when she could safely articulate the words.

"Look, why don't we just forget—" She heard the anger building in his voice.

"Oh, no you don't!" she quickly interrupted him. "The entire day is yours if you want it."

"What about Herman?" He said the other man's name like a curse and she chuckled.

"Henry," she automatically corrected. Then she quickly added, "You know I'm not interested in Henry."

"Then why did you throw him in my face the other night?"

His voice evidenced his displeasure. She bet he was scowling into the phone and scratching his hair-covered chin in frustration.

"Because you needed me to," she easily responded. "Apparently, he did the trick."

"Apparently," he grudgingly admitted. "What happened when he took you home?"

"What usually happens when a man takes a woman home," she couldn't resist teasing.

"Marcy…" His voice held a warning.

"You know nothing happened between us," she softly scolded and smiled when he sighed audibly in relief. "You didn't like seeing me with him, did you?"

"No," he shortly yet decisively responded. "Did he kiss you good-night?"

"Nathan," she chided, "I'm not the kiss-and-tell kind of girl."

"Marcy…"

"You're jealous." She laughed happily. "I think I like that."

"Did he?" Nathan persisted, waiting impatiently for an answer.

"Of course he didn't kiss me," she softly promised, deciding to stop torturing him. "I'm saving all my kisses for you, handsome."

"Good," he approved, and she laughed.

"You don't want me to see him again?"

"You *won't* see him again," he firmly stated.

"Or any other man, except you?"

"No other man but me," he ordered, and her eyes closed momentarily in triumph.

"You want exclusivity, then?" She paused, and when he didn't answer she relented. "What do you have in mind for today?"

"Let's play it by ear."

"I love spontaneity," she agreed brightly, giving up all pretense of not being happy he had called her.

"Yes, I've noticed," he dryly responded. "I'll pick you up in…an hour or is that too early?"

"It's perfect. I'll be ready," she promised before ringing off. She suddenly stood up, lifted her hands in triumph and shouted in glee.

"Ms. Johnson, are you all right?" the receptionist asked, coming through her door unannounced.

"Fabulous!" Marcy hugged her and then sprinted back to her desk, flopped down in her chair twirling around. "Oh, Peggy?" She halted the other woman as she prepared to leave.

"Yes, ma'am?"

"Clear all my appointments for the rest of the day, and ask Sally if she can take my three o'clock meeting with Fisher," Marcy ordered.

"Yes, ma'am, but you do have a meeting with Robert Brown at two o'clock," she reminded.

"Oh, no." She had been courting him for months. "I'll call him myself," she decided, picking up the phone as the other woman left her alone.

She would persuade Mr. Brown to reschedule because money or no, she wasn't going to cancel on Nathan. She had worked too hard to get that stubborn, wonderful, intriguing man to admit she was important to him. She couldn't wait to see what he had planned for her today— or to show him what she had planned for him tonight.

Exactly an hour later, Nathan strolled into Marcy's office looking more handsome than ever dressed casually in dark jeans, a black leather jacket and black shirt.

His appreciative eyes raked her from head to toe. She was dressed in a plum pantsuit, and her thick mane of hair was carelessly piled high on her head in thick wavy ringlets. Her plum lips curved slightly at the sight of him and sent painful desire shooting into his loins. She was the most beautiful woman he had ever laid eyes on, and she was his.

"Hi, handsome. Right on time," she gaily responded, walking from behind her desk.

"I believe in being punctual."

Lord, she looked great. Couldn't she ever look anything less than stunning? His eyes were hungry for the sight of her. Had it only been two days since he had seen her last? It had seemed like an eternity.

"Did you miss me?" She lightly fingered the sleeve of his biker jacket.

"Marcy, I'm here," he sardonically reminded.

"I know, and I'm glad you are, but did you miss me?" She refused to relent, trailing her hand up his leather-clad arm.

"Yes, I missed you." He snapped the words as his hands lightly touched her waist. "Satisfied?"

"You don't have to bite my head off." She smiled, cradling his face in her hands. "I missed you, too," she whis-

pered. They both levitated toward each other as if drawn
by invisible strings. "Terribly."

She barely got the words out before their lips met in
an exploratory and then consuming kiss. He feasted on
her lips as if he were a starving man being unexpectedly
given a feast. Why did she have to taste so good? Why did
she have to feel so good in his arms? He never wanted to
let her go. He wanted to drown in her softness and scent.

"Hugo will never kiss you like that," he promised
against her lips.

"Henry," she corrected. At his frown, she laughed. "Of
course he won't."

He smiled triumphantly before capturing her mouth
again in a decadent embrace she prayed would never end.
The thought of the other man kissing her as he was filled
him with rage and the fact that he hadn't imbued him with
strength.

Marcy felt positively scorched when his lips continued
their thorough devastation of hers. Her bones turned to
liquid as his tongue sought, encountered and consumed
hers. How long they kissed neither knew. A kiss would
soon not be enough to assuage the flames licking through
every part of their bodies—this they both realized and ac-
cordingly reluctantly ended their kiss.

When he pulled away, she still held his face in her
hands; his were around her waist. She slowly opened her
eyes and stared at him helplessly, unable to speak, barely
able to breathe.

"I didn't want to care about you," he suddenly confessed, troubled eyes staring deeply into hers.

"Do you care?" Her heart somersaulted at his words as
her fingers caressed his cheekbones.

"I'm afraid I do." He nearly groaned as her arms twined

around his neck and she pressed her shapely length closer to his.

"Why afraid?" Her expression bore puzzlement. "Why not glad?"

"Marcy…" He paused, searching for words, and she did something that was hard for her—remained silent. "I can't explain so you'll understand," he finished, trailing his fingers up her back and then back down.

"Then don't. Just be with me," she magnanimously offered, shuddering at his actions.

"I want to," he admitted, eyes darkening as she began tracing the outline of his lower lip with her thumb. *For as long as I'm able to.*

"Then do." She acted as if it was the easiest and most natural thing in the world.

"I wish it was that simple." His eyes grew distant and disturbed.

"It is," she promised, kissing him lightly. Then, in a tone designed to lighten his mood, she asked, "What fabulous place are you taking me to?"

"It's a surprise," he said and smiled. She always knew when to back off. Her hands moved from his face to his shoulders, down his arms to grasp his hands.

"I love surprises." She smiled, pleased that the forlorn look had almost completely disappeared from his eyes. "Am I dressed all right?"

"You're always dressed perfectly," he flattered. "Let's go." He brought her hands to his lips and then released one as he led her out of the office into the elevator.

God help him he was going to destroy her, and the only way he could possibly prevent it was to cut her loose now, walk out of her life and never see her again; unfortunately, that was the one thing he simply couldn't bring himself to contemplate—let alone accomplish.

Chapter 9

When Nathan stopped the car in front of his parents' Rochester home, Marcy turned to stare at him in shock. "You brought me to your parents' house?"

"Do you mind?" He watched her closely.

"No, I love your parents and Nicole. I'm just surprised," she explained.

He smiled at her before getting out and opening the car door for her. "Well, Mom has been on me for not spending enough time with them, and I agreed to come for the afternoon. Afterward, I thought we could catch the New York game."

"You have tickets?" He laughed at her obvious excitement as he helped her from the car.

"Floor seats." He reached in his breast pocket and showed them to her. "It's the least I can do for making you miss the game the other night."

"How did you get these?" She wanted to know, holding on to the tickets as if they were gold.

"I have contacts," he whispered, prying the tickets from her fingers and placing them back in his pocket.

"I can't wait."

"Really?" It was ludicrous how much he had wanted to please her.

"Really," she promised, impulsively reaching up and kissing him deeply just as the door opened to reveal his parents. He could see the wheels turning in his mother's head as she watched them with glee evident on her face.

"Uh-oh, now you've done it." Nathan placed an arm around her waist.

"Sorry," she whispered, moving close to his side as she reached out and embraced his parents.

"Marcy, it is wonderful to see you again—especially with Nathan." Linda kissed her cheek warmly.

"It's nice to see both of you again Mr. and Mrs. Carter," Marcy said and smiled.

"We're almost family," Linda predicted, winking at her son's scowl. "It's Linda and Lincoln," she corrected.

"Yes, ma'am," Marcy agreed.

Linda frowned disapprovingly at her son. "It's about time you showed up."

"Mom, I'm here now." Nathan sighed. "Ouch!" he complained as she pinched his ear in reproof.

Marcy hid a laugh behind her hand as Lincoln led her into the house, followed closely by Nathan and Linda.

"When will you learn?" Lincoln laughed at Nathan, who was still being scolded by his mother.

"Where's Nicole?" Marcy asked.

"Upstairs. She'll be down soon," Lincoln answered as they went into the living room with him.

"Are you going to admonish me the entire time I'm here?" Nathan rubbed his ear as he sat beside Marcy.

"I should, but I don't want Marcy to think I'm too hard on my children." Linda threatened his other ear with her fingers and he moved away from her and that much closer to Marcy.

"Oh, don't mind me." Marcy smiled as Linda sat on the arm of her husband's chair and his arm went around her waist.

"Thanks for the help." Nathan frowned at her.

"Any time." She chuckled.

"I think I'm bleeding," Nathan complained.

"Let me see." Marcy carefully inspected his ear. "No, you're not," she assured him.

"Well, it feels like it," he continued to grumble.

"It serves you right, staying away from your family for so long. I have never—" Linda's eyes sparkled as she began her good-natured tirade.

"Hi, everyone." Nicole breezed in, interrupting her mother.

"Saved at last!" Nathan's eyes turned heavenward at his sister's entrance.

"What have I missed?" Nicole laughed as she curled her frame into the chair opposite her father.

"Your mother was just reprimanding your brother." Lincoln chuckled and then grimaced as his wife pinched his arm in retaliation.

"Ah, the usual, then." Nicole smiled as her father rubbed his arm and Nathan rubbed his ear.

"Has anyone heard from the newlyweds?" Nathan asked to get his mother's mind on something other than him.

"Tash and Damien are tucked away in wedded bliss," Nicole said and smiled. "I don't think we'll be hearing from them any time soon."

"There's nothing like finding the right person to share your life with." Linda glanced from her son to Marcy.

"Natasha and Damien certainly are perfect for each other," Marcy agreed around a smile.

"They're not the only ones," Linda slyly predicted.

"Momma, whatever do you mean?" Nicole innocently asked and fought against hysterical laughter as Nathan shot her a killing look.

"I'm starving. Is lunch ready?" Nathan abruptly stood.

"This one, Marcy. He has an appetite that is endless," Linda responded as they walked into the dining room. "The woman who marries him will have to own stock in a grocery store." She smiled knowingly. "But you'll soon find out."

"Thanks for the tip." Marcy's humor increased at Nathan's scowl as they were seated around the table.

"Can I help you bring in the food, Linda?" Marcy asked, preparing to get up.

"No, no. You sit and entertain Nathan and Lincoln. Nicole will help me." She glanced at her youngest, who sighed and rose to obey.

"Dad, can't you do something with Mom?" Nathan asked when they were alone.

"Like what?" His father smiled at his son and at Marcy, who was trying unsuccessfully to hide her amusement.

"Convince her that at thirty-one I am capable of leading my own life," Nathan exasperatedly suggested.

"Ha! I'd rather fight ten angry tigers than to interfere with your mother once she has set her mind to something." Lincoln negatively shook his head.

"And you are not helping the matter, either." Nathan shot Marcy a stern look as she chuckled uncontrollably.

"I'm sorry." She giggled, and Lincoln joined her. Soon

the two were laughing heartily while Nathan sighed in annoyance.

A few minutes later, steaming food covered the table, and Nicole and Linda reseated themselves. Soon, everyone's plate was filled to overflowing at Linda's insistence.

"Mmm, everything smells wonderful." Marcy smiled as she picked up her fork.

"There's nothing like Mom's cooking," Nathan flattered, hoping to keep his mother's mind on food and off of him for a few minutes at least.

"Everyone dig in," Lincoln ordered, picking up his fork.

"When you're married, you'll say the same thing about your wife's cooking," Linda promised and chuckled as her son remained noticeably silent.

Nicole winked at Marcy before teasing her brother, "I bet you've left a string of broken hearts behind in Washington."

"Hardly. I've been working," Nathan denied, placing a piece of roast into his mouth, wishing everyone would follow suit and cut the annoying chatter.

"Your job is too demanding," Linda disapproved.

"Yes, it is, but I knew that when I signed on," Nathan agreed, spearing a potato with his fork.

"Perhaps it is time to reevaluate anything that keeps you away from your family for so long," Linda suggested.

"Linda, leave Nathan alone." Lincoln gently touched her hand.

"This pot roast is delicious." Marcy tried to divert Linda's attention.

"Thank you. It's in the marinade," she replied. Nicole and Lincoln stifled grins behind their hands. She always said that about every type of meat she cooked.

"What are you two snickering—" Linda's voice halted as the phone began ringing.

"I'll get it." Nicole excused herself and walked into the hall to answer the phone. "Hello."

"May I speak with Ms. Nicole Carter, please," an unfamiliar, pleasing, deep male voice asked.

"This is Nicole," she responded, sitting down on a bench.

"Ms. Carter, this is Alexander James."

"Really?" Her heart was suddenly racing in excitement.

"Really." His voice held a hint of humor.

Her eyes widened in awe. "*The* Alexander James?"

"The only one that I know of," he said and chuckled.

"Mr. James, I can't wait to be with you. I mean to get to know you. I mean…" She was babbling like an idiot, and she was helpless to stop herself. *She was talking to Alexander James!*

"Stop while you're ahead, Ms. Carter," he dryly suggested, and she wondered if he was smiling.

"Nicole," she breathlessly offered, placing a hand over her thudding heart.

"I just wanted to call and congratulate you on beating out some stiff competition and let you know I'll be sending you an info package later this week." He was cool and professional.

"Thank you. I'll be watching for it," she assured him.

"Please let the office know if you don't receive it next week."

"I will."

"We'll see you in about a month, then…Nicole."

"I look forward to it, Mr. James." She was proud her voice didn't shake.

"Alex," he contradicted after a brief pause.

"Alex," she happily repeated and was somewhat sad when he rang off without any further comment.

"Nicole, are you going to finish your lunch?" Her mother's voice rang out.

"Yes, Momma, I'm coming." She set the phone down and rejoined her family.

"Who was that?" Lincoln asked.

"Alexander James." Nicole grinned happily.

"The man you'll be working for in Paris?" her mother asked.

"Yes, he called to congratulate me and let me know he was sending me some information," she said and took a necessary sip of her water.

"That was nice of him." Marcy smiled. "I'm sure you can't wait to get there."

"No, I can't," she agreed. This was the opportunity of a lifetime, and she couldn't wait to make her mark upon the fashion world.

"All of my children are deserting me." Linda sadly shook her head.

"Oh, Momma." Nicole and Nathan sighed together.

"It's all right. It is a mother's lot in life," she bemoaned.

"It's a fabulous opportunity for Nicole," Marcy gently stated, and Nicole shot her a grateful smile.

"I know. I won't stand in her way," Linda promised.

"You've been very supportive, and I appreciate it." Nicole blew her a kiss.

"Because I'm so proud of you." Linda beamed. "To think my little girl will soon be a famous fashion designer."

"She's already promised me a suit," Marcy chimed in.

"And I'll deliver," Nicole promised.

"Like you need any more clothes," Nathan teased.

"Son," Lincoln said and chuckled, "don't you know that a woman can never have enough clothes?"

"I have taught him well." Linda glanced lovingly at

Lincoln. "I wished I could say the same for my son." she turned her pointed gaze toward Nathan.

"What do you mean, Mom?" Nathan sighed.

"Well, for one thing, it's a disgrace you living in a hotel when we have all this room." Linda waved her hand and shook her head in admonishment.

"I explained that to you. Even though I am on vacation, there are still things I have to do for work." Nathan reiterated his trumped-up reason for not staying with his family.

"I know, I know, but still—" Linda began.

"Mrs. Carter..." Marcy received a stern look. "I'm sorry, Linda," Marcy corrected. "I would love your recipe for this roast."

"I'll give it to you before you leave. After all, you're almost family." She glanced suggestively at Nathan, who shook his head helplessly while everyone else laughed.

"Don't be too hard on your mother, son. She only wants to see you happy." Lincoln patted his son on the back as they walked outside after lunch.

"I know." Nathan sighed.

"What's wrong?" Lincoln asked as they stopped. He could feel the frustration and unhappiness oozing from him.

"It's nothing." Nathan shook his head and then at his father's concerned face. "Dad, I'm just...things are just... very complicated right now."

"You mean with Marcy?" His father leaned against the wooden fence.

"Yes, she's..." Nathan paused at a loss for words.

"What? Beautiful, intelligent, sexy?"

"She's all those things. She's also stubborn and infuriating." Nathan smiled because in Marcy those characteristics were attributes not flaws.

"What woman isn't?" Lincoln chuckled. "She cares about you, son."

"I know." His smile faded. "I wish she didn't."

Lincoln frowned. "Why?"

"It's…" He faltered again.

"Complicated," Lincoln supplied the word.

"Yes," he said and sighed heavily. "I know I'm not making any sense."

"Son, when a woman is involved, a man never makes any sense," his father advised. "Marcy is a good woman."

"I know she is," Nathan readily agreed, stuffing his hands into his jacket pockets.

"You were jealous when she brought that other man to dinner," Lincoln reminded.

"I was. Yes," Nathan agreed, his lips thinning at the memory of her with Herbert.

"You like her."

"Very much." Nathan didn't bother to deny it.

"Do you want to see her with someone else?" Nathan's stomach lurched at his father's question.

"No," he answered quickly. "No, I don't."

"Then what's holding you back?"

Nathan glanced at his father; it was clear he didn't understand his dilemma. How could he? No one knew he'd soon be on the other side of the world battling against insurgents as he tried to rescue the U.S. envoy and his aides and ensure that they all made it back home safely.

"Obligations and duty," he said, and sighed after a long pause.

"Those are important to a man, but there's one thing that's even more important," his father advised.

"What's that?"

"Love." Lincoln placed an arm around his son's shoulders. "Love for a good woman and love of a good woman—nothing else compares to that."

Nathan shrugged. "Maybe one day…"

"One day soon if your mother and Marcy's mother have anything to say about it." His father smiled.

"They are adamant about us getting together, aren't they?" Nathan's brow furrowed.

"Yes, but only because they know it's what you both want." Lincoln's smile widened as his son's frown increased.

"Who says I want Marcy?"

"One very important person whose opinion you can't run away from no matter how hard you try."

Nathan sighed. "Mom?"

"No, son—you," his father gently corrected, walking off and leaving him alone to contemplate his wise words.

"So, Nicole, tell me more about that phone call from Alexander James," Marcy said as they sat in the living room.

"There's not much to tell." Nicole shrugged.

"You seem—" she paused, searching for the correct words "—intrigued by him."

"By his business acumen," Nicole corrected. "He runs one of the biggest, most successful fashion houses in Paris. Naturally, I can't wait to learn from him."

"Paris is the city of love," Marcy reminded with a wide smile.

"I'm going there for my career, Marcy," Nicole firmly countered. "Besides, I'm sure Alex will work me so hard that I won't have time to think about anything else."

"Alex, huh?"

"Alexander," Nicole amended.

"Are you as nonchalant as you appear?"

"Of course I am." At Marcy's raised eyebrow, she continued, "He seemed really nice on the phone, but I'm definitely not thinking about romance—especially not with my boss."

"Well, I've learned to expect the unexpected." Marcy chuckled. "The last thing I expected was to open my front door and find your brother standing there, or that he would knock me for a 360 degree loop without even trying."

Nicole shook her head at her friend but remained silent. She was focused on her career, not on romance with anyone, especially not Alexander James. She was going to Paris to learn from a great designer, work her fingers to the bones and spread her wings. The very idea of engaging in an office romance was out of the question—especially with the owner of the company.

"Marcy, I don't want you to think I'm a prying mother." Linda entered the living room from the kitchen, wiping her hands on her apron.

"Heaven forbid," Nicole teased.

"You be quiet." Linda waved a warning finger at her youngest as she sat beside Marcy on the sofa.

"I don't think you're interfering," Marcy assured. "I think you love your children very much and just want to see them happy."

"Finally, a sensible perspective." Linda beamed at her, taking her hands in hers. "I know in my heart you can make my son happy."

"Thank you. I think so, too," Marcy agreed.

"What's the problem, then?"

"Nathan just needs a little time to get used to the idea of having someone special in his life," Marcy predicted.

"Time? That boy doesn't need any time. He needs to open his eyes and smell the coffee," Linda emphasized.

Marcy leaned closer and conspiratorially whispered,

"Well, you know that and I know that, but how are we going to convince him of that?"

"You did well the other night by bringing a date to dinner," Nicole praised.

"Nathan was livid." Linda chuckled at the memory.

"I know." Marcy's chuckle quickly turned into a full-blown laugh.

"Now he realizes he could easily have competition," Nicole chimed in.

"He knows he doesn't have any competition from Henry or any other man," Marcy confessed.

"Well—" Nicole shrugged "—it doesn't hurt him to *think* that he might."

"I think I tortured him enough with Henry," Marcy decided. "Why are men so stubborn?"

"They are all the same—clinging to their bachelorhood like a badge of honor, forcing us to drag them kicking and screaming into love," Linda wisely stated, and they all shook their heads in agreement.

About thirty minutes later, Nathan returned from a long walk to find the women sitting on the sofa talking and laughing like lifelong cohorts. One look at Marcy and Nathan didn't have to ask what they had been conspiring about.

"Lunch was great Mom, but Marcy and I have to be leaving." Nathan held out a hand to Marcy, who stood and walked toward him.

"Leaving? You just got here!" Linda complained.

"I'm sorry. I promised to take Marcy to a game." Any objection Linda was about to make died on her lips at her son's words.

"That's wonderful." She had no interest in basketball,

but at least they were going together. "You two go and enjoy each other."

Nathan sighed heavily before kissing her cheek. "I'll see you all later."

"Thanks for having me." Marcy waved as they left.

"Come back soon, Marcy."

"I will," Marcy agreed over her shoulder.

"They are a lovely couple, aren't they?" Linda smiled as she watched the two of them leave.

"Yes, they are," Nicole agreed and received a smile.

"Linda…" Lincoln's eyebrow rose in warning.

"I'm just saying." Linda held up her hands in mock surrender. "I have to go and call Margaret." She quickly walked off, ignoring the shaking heads of her husband and daughter.

She could already picture the vision Marcy would make as she walked down the aisle toward her eldest child.

Chapter 10

"Let me drive," Marcy suggested once they made it outside. "You look like you could use the time to think."

"Thanks." He handed her the keys with gratitude, slumping in the passenger seat with a thoughtful frown on his face.

"Your mother meant well, Nathan," she softly interrupted his thoughts as they drove off.

"I know." He sighed, glancing at her, absently touching her hair.

His thoughts replayed the conversation with his father. How true his observations had been; he did want Marcy very much. He wanted to lose himself in her—to leave all his troubles behind until he could think of nothing but her. He wanted to merge his body with hers so completely that he never found his way out again. Everything the world had to offer was reflected in her eyes when she looked at him as if he was the most important person in her life.

How had he existed thirty-one years without her? How could he possibly go on another second if she wasn't with him completely?

Marcy fought for concentration as his fingers trailed from her brow to the end of her hair. "I—um…" She paused to swallow the lump in her throat. "Do you really want to go to the game?"

"No, not really."

"Then where?"

"You're not upset?" She felt him staring at her and glanced at him briefly before returning her attention to the road.

"No." She negatively shook her head, causing strands of her hair to brush over his fingers. "I don't care where we go, Nathan. I just want to be with you."

"You're very special," he spoke softly to himself and reached out and lightly fingered a ringlet of hair at her cheek.

"Thank you." She trembled at his touch. "Where to?"

He considered her question carefully. He knew what he wanted and that she wanted the same thing. He had fought the attraction between them because he didn't want to hurt her; he still didn't. There was, however, one way they could be together and that was if… He paused and contemplated long and hard before completing his thought, *If he left the unit.* Was he ready to do that? Did he have any other choice if he wanted a life with the incomparable woman sitting next to him?

"Nathan?" She glanced at him briefly before returning her attention to the road.

"Let's go to my place," he finally answered, trailing a finger down her smooth cheek and smiling at her gasp of surprise.

"Your place?" She turned to stare at him again to make sure she had heard him correctly.

"Isn't that what you want?" His finger moved to circle her earlobe.

"Yes." She sighed. "Very much."

"So do I." His voice held resignation and barely repressed longing. "I'm tired of fighting it…you…us."

"Your place it is, then," she breathlessly agreed. Her heartbeat accelerated at the thought of finally making love to him. "Can I ask you one thing?"

"What?" His fingers fisted in her hair, and she let out her breath on a sigh.

"Please stop touching me—for now," she pleaded.

"For now," he agreed, smiling slightly before removing his hand and sitting back in his seat. "But when we get to my place, I'm going to touch and taste every inch of you," he seductively promised.

She gasped in anticipation but remained silent, though her foot depressed the accelerator causing the car to speed up considerably.

A short while later when they entered his suite, he paused long enough to place a do not disturb sign on the door before closing it firmly. He glanced at her, and she quickly looked away and walked farther into the room.

"You're nervous," he noted as he took her coat and laid it over a chair with his own before turning her to face him.

"Yes, I'm sorry," she admitted, twisting her hands before realizing what she was doing and stopping.

"Don't be. It's exciting." He touched her cheek lightly before turning to pick up the phone. "I'll order some champagne."

"No, I don't want any champagne." Her hand on his arm halted him.

"No?" And at her negative nod, his fingers deftly unbuttoned and then removed her suit jacket, revealing only a black lace chemise underneath. "What do you want?"

"I want you, Nathan," she informed him, shivering as his hands slid down her bare arms.

"I want you, too," he admitted on a growl. Damn his good intentions. He had tried to stay away from her—he really had, but she was right; this was inevitable.

"Show me how much," she whispered against his mouth and smiled as he effortlessly picked her up, carried her to the bedroom and gently laid her on the bed.

"I won't hurt you," he promised as he slid her pants and shoes off. He prayed he was telling her the truth. He wouldn't think about having to leave her soon; he'd work it out—somehow.

"I know," she whispered as he lay down beside her.

His mouth toyed with hers as his hands pulled the thin straps of her camisole down until it hung limply on her arms. His lips and teeth trailed over her exposed flesh until she was breathing heavily. His hands moved down to still her hips as they moved restlessly against his, and then his rapacious mouth captured hers again.

Unsteady hands unbuttoned his shirt and spread it open across his muscled chest. She had to touch him; she needed to touch him. She felt his quick intake of breath as her hands tentatively explored his hard naked flesh. His mouth grew more insistent on hers. He released her lips to bury his face in her hair as he fought for some semblance of control. He had to make this special for her, not take her like a wild stallion as his body longed for him to do.

Her hands moved to his back as his mouth slid down her neck. His hands slowly, purposefully pulled the camisole down, exposing her firm and swollen breasts. His lips lightly tasted the flesh his hands had uncovered, tongue flicking lightly over one distended nub and then the other. He felt and heard her gasp as he gently took a nipple between his teeth, teasing until it was button hard before sucking her breast into his hot mouth and feasting as if he were a starving man.

Her eyes closed, and she moaned a maddening sound and her hands moved behind his head, pressing him closer as he touched her at will, devastating her. He slowly teased her skin with wet openmouthed kisses down her body, lingering at her flat stomach while his fingers gently slid to the inside of a silky thigh before moving to touch her intimately. She convulsed as searing heat and pleasure such as she had never known before engulfed her. Her hands grasped the bedspread, her head lolled from side to side and she shattered into a million pieces.

As her breathing slowed somewhat, all her dazed mind could register was that she felt wonderful and free. She didn't know what Nathan had done to her, but she knew she couldn't possibly experience anything like it again. He proved her wrong as his mouth and tongue replaced his hand, and he destroyed her until she was screaming and groaning in shocked pleasure, her hips lifting in wanton invitation to his seeking mouth.

She didn't realize he shifted off her momentarily to remove his pants and place on protection, and she was still trembling, eyes closed as his mouth snaked its way back up her quivering flesh until it was level with her own.

"Marcy, open your eyes," he whispered, and she fought to obey until she stared at him. "I need you."

"Take me," she breathlessly offered when she could speak before hungry lips imbibed hers.

She felt hands on her hips lift her, and then he slowly gently slipped into her, centimeter by centimeter, inch by wonderful inch. She gasped at the momentary sharp pain caused by the invasion of his hard warmth. He remained motionless for several seconds, only moving when she arched up bringing him deeper. He fought to control himself as she absorbed him, welcomed him and perfectly surrounded him. He shook with the effort to be gentle; she was so tight and felt so good, he thought he would die from pleasure. When finally he was completely within her pulsing depths, he began to move gently yet urgently. Her body met every thrust, and she whimpered in astonishment and pleasure against his mouth. By sheer will, he forced himself to go slowly as he took her soaring.

"God, you feel so good," he groaned into her ear before his hot mouth took up residence in the crook of her softly scented neck. "Perfect."

She would have spoken, but she couldn't articulate. She couldn't breathe or think. All she was capable of doing was holding on to her lover as they raced toward sweet fulfillment.

Unable to help himself, he started to move faster, more purposefully, and she sprinted with him toward what she didn't know. She was on the verge of dying from pleasure, and he held them both on that slippery ledge between reason and sanity for countless thrilling moments before finally thrusting them over the precipice into utter madness.

Afterward, lying in Nathan's arms, their labored breathing slowly returned to normal. "Mmm, that was delicious." Marcy sighed, kissing his neck.

"It was new," he seriously replied, entangling his fingers in her thick hair as she kissed his chest. He had never felt this way before.

"In a good way?" she spoke against his flesh.

"In the best way," he agreed, pulling her mouth up to meet his. Her soft, curvaceous body half lay across his as he feasted on her lips. "You're not sorry?"

"How could you ask me that?" she chided, tracing the outline of his lower lip with her tongue, which he captured with his teeth and used to bring her mouth back to his. God, he could kiss her forever and never tire of it.

"Marcy." He groaned her name.

"Why did you fight so hard against something so wonderful?" she asked when she could speak and felt him sigh heavily.

"My life is such a mess right now," he slowly answered.

"How so?" She propped her chin on his chest to gaze adoringly at him.

"I'm sorry, but I can't tell you." He braced for anger. He didn't want to keep anything from her, but while he was still bound to his unit, he had to because his oath of allegiance and secrecy was something he could never break, not even for her.

"I'll wait until you can, then," she calmly responded.

"You're not angry?"

"How can I be angry after you just made me feel so marvelous?" She kissed his lips lightly, and his hands tangled in her hair, holding it away from her gorgeous, satisfied face.

"You're so special," he again marveled, pulling her fully on top of him.

"As long as there's no one else," she absurdly responded as she slid her body along his hard length, enjoying the differences in textures.

"There is no one else for me except you," he solemnly swore.

Her heart nearly burst at his admission. "Then I can wait until you can tell me what's bothering you." She curled against him. "Nathan?"

"Hmm?"

"Was I all right?" She held her breath for his answer.

"No." Her head snapped up at his soft response.

"No?" she responded, crushed. "What could I have...?"

"Marcy, there aren't any words to describe how wonderful it was to love you," he interrupted.

"Really?" All apprehension vanished at his words.

"Really." He kissed her lips softly, and she snuggled back against his chest, content.

He held her close, hands running down her bare satiny back. She was wonderful; he didn't deserve her, yet here she was with him, saying and doing all the right things. For the first time in his life, he hated his job—hated anything that would take him away from her.

She sighed contentedly; she couldn't help herself. How long had she dreamed of this moment? All of her life and as beautiful as her dreams had been, the reality had far surpassed them. She pressed her lips to his chest and felt the strong beating of his heart—a heart that she knew belonged to her now. He was everything she wanted, everything she needed, and she had no intention of ever letting him go.

She had sapped his strength, yet he felt desire stirring in him again—desire and another strong emotion he was loath to name. His fingers entangled in her hair and pulled her head up until their eyes were level.

"I want you again." He spoke against her lips.

"I want you, too—always," she whispered.

"I should let you rest."

"I don't want to rest." She managed to get the words out before his mouth engulfed hers, and he simultaneously rolled her beneath him.

She protested when he rolled away for a second to place on a condom, but he was soon back, his wonderfully hard body pinning hers to the mattress. She gasped in pleasure when without preamble his body hungrily joined with hers. He took her greedily this time, wanting to be absorbed by her, needing to possess her wildly for fear she would disappear if he didn't. She met him, matched him; her limbs pulled him tighter, her nails raked down his rippling back as his body continued to bombard hers, and all too soon, she began shaking violently as a blinding orgasm hit. He released her lips to bury his face in her hair, and she heard him call her name out hoarsely as he emptied himself into her. She held him tight as he trembled against her before finally stilling, breathing heavy against her neck.

She had always known when she fell in love that it would be completely, but she'd never expected to fall so hard this fast. She was shaking not from cold but from the knowledge that she was desperately in love with Nathan. This was what she had waited her entire life to experience; he was the man she had been placed on this earth for. She loved him, and there was no doubt in her mind now that he loved her, too.

She wanted to tell him how she felt, but she held back for now because she didn't think he was ready to hear it. He needed to acknowledge his feelings for her first. Once he did, she'd shout her love for him from the rooftops; she couldn't wait for that day to come.

Nathan lightly rubbed Marcy's back as she slept, her warm soft body curled around his. He knew he'd never feel this content again without her lying beside him. He loved her with his entire heart. His fingers stilled at his monumental silent admission. *He loved Marcy.* He loved her with everything that he was.

He wanted to wake her and tell her but knew he couldn't—yet. When what he now knew was going to be his last mission was over, once he had freed himself from his duty and obligations to his country, when he was able to be completely honest with her, then he would tell her and that day couldn't come soon enough for him.

Marcy stirred and opened drowsy eyes when Nathan's cell phone began incessantly ringing. It was pitch-black in the room save for the city lights shining through the partially opened drapes at the windows.

"Forget about it," she ordered, burying her face into his chest as he stirred.

"I can't." He reluctantly extricated himself from her warm limbs and walked over to his jacket to retrieve the offending instrument. She sighed, annoyed, yet sleepily she enjoyed the view of his chiseled naked body.

"Carter," he snapped. "Yeah." He glanced at her and walked into the hallway before resuming his conversation.

"Who was that?" she asked when he returned minutes later.

"Business," he shortly replied, scratching his chin.

"I thought you were on vacation?" She smoothed her hair out of her eyes as she watched him. He seemed tense. Had the call been bad news? What was suddenly bothering him?

"I told you that I'm never really free from my job." His voice sounded strange—strained.

"Come back to me." She sat up and opened her arms in welcome.

"Marcy…" He stayed where he was, several feet away from her.

Damn! Everything was nearly set for his deployment. They had located the camp where they believed the abductees were being held; they were just waiting for satellite confirmation. Once they had it, he'd be on his way to Yemen—and away from Marcy.

"Nathan." She unabashedly got up and came to him,

taking him into her arms, and he crushed her to him. "Was it bad news?"

He raised his head to stare at the torture evident in his eyes, "Yes, no…" His voice trailed off.

Then before she could ask what was wrong, he kissed her desperately and held her as if he would be lost without her. Somehow they were back on the bed, and his hands, lips and body caressed her frantically trying to absorb the feel and taste of her. He seemed rushed, almost desperate. She wanted him to confide in her, but he seemed to need this from her more than words, so she gave him everything she had to give and more.

He rolled until she was on top of him and sat up with her sitting in his lap. Without releasing her, somehow he managed to don a condom. Their lips never lost contact as his hands moved to her hips, lifting her slightly and then bringing her back down to engulf his hardness. Their bodies melted together—made for each other. Their lips echoed the frenzied movements of their bodies as they quivered, trembled and held each other tight.

There was no talking with words, but there was moaning, gasping and sighing as they greedily gave and took all—everything, until he collapsed back against the pillows, taking her with him, still holding her tight—daring anything or anyone to try and take her from him.

In the morning Marcy slowly awoke with a smile on her lips. As her groggy mind began to function, she remembered why she was so happy; turning her head, she encountered an empty space where Nathan had been. She heard the shower running and got out of bed, stretched like a contented cat and walked over to the bathroom. She stood watching the fuzzy outline of Nathan's splendid body through the glass of the stall before she tiptoed over, quietly slid open the door and got into the shower with him.

"Marcy," he groaned as her arms went around him from behind.

"Good morning," she whispered, kissing his wet back until he turned around and captured her lips with his.

"Good morning," he moaned against her mouth. "You're hair's getting wet."

"I don't care." She dismissed his words as her long tresses were pelted with warm water. She ran her hands up and down his arms, and her eyes focused on his left biceps. "I didn't figure you for the tattoo type."

"I'm not really."

"Musical notes?" She raised an eyebrow. "Did you used to be a singer?" He made a comical face and laughed at her suggestion, and she joined him.

"If you heard me sing, you'd never suspect that." The tattoo had been specially chosen for his unit for its banality—who would imagine an elite commando would have such a tattoo? "I got it on a dare."

"From a woman?"

He chuckled. "No, some guys I work with." Everyone in his team had the same tattoo and how they had moaned about getting it—each wanted something fiercer, manlier.

"I like it." She traced her tongue over one of the symbols.

"Yeah?" He liked it, too, now that she was caressing it.

"Mmm-hmm—" her mouth moved to his chest "—it makes you seem unpredictable and a little dangerous."

His fingers tangled in her hair. "Just a little?"

"Just the right amount." Sultry eyes met his blazing ones.

"Let me show you how dangerous I can be." His mouth

swooped down to capture hers, but she avoided him. "What?"

"Are you okay?" She fingered his slightly stubbly cheek.

"That's usually the man's line the morning after," he quipped, soapy hands trailing over her.

"You know why I asked that." She sighed as his hands moved to her breasts then low on her stomach. "You seemed upset by that phone call last night."

"I'm fine," he assured, caressing her mouth with his.

"You didn't seem fine last night," she persisted. "Nathan, tell me—" Her words were cut off as his mouth pinned to hers.

His hands moved to her hips, yanking until her legs encircled his waist, and he slipped familiarly and easily into her, backing her against a nearby white tile wall. His hot body slid maddeningly against hers; her water-slicked limbs pulled him closer. Water continued to pelt them as he filled her and she surrounded him. God, she wouldn't have believed a body could withstand such intense pleasure over and over again; yet, as he had shown her last night and was expertly demonstrating again, it could.

Their mouths hungrily feasted on each other's before he released her lips to taste the slick skin of her shoulders and neck before seeking out her lips again. She was drowning, but she didn't care. His hands pulled her hips tighter against his, and her nails traveled down his rippling back to his taut butt pressing him closer and closer.

He took her, they took each other, until all questions he couldn't answer were forgotten—everything was forgotten except the unbelievable pleasure mounting within and the unvoiced love overflowing from both of their hearts.

Marcy floated through the day at work having gotten there only an hour ago after she and Nathan had made love again. God, he was a fantastic lover, or was it the fact that she was in love with him that made what they had shared so special? She suspected it was a little of both.

She was deliriously happy, but she couldn't shake the feeling that something was troubling her man; since that phone call last night, he had changed, become more— brooding? However, every time she had tried to question him, he had silenced her most effectively and pleasantly. She would get it out of him eventually; she was after all known for her tenacity.

Her phone rang, and she picked it up hoping it was the object of her thoughts. "Marcy Johnson."

"Hello, Marcy."

"Hi, Natasha. How's married life?"

"Wonderful." She sighed happily.

"How's my brother?"

"Wonderful." Natasha's voice grew even dreamier—if that were possible.

"I am *totally* jealous." Marcy chuckled.

"Don't be. Your turn will come soon," Natasha predicted.

"I'm working on it," Marcy softly informed.

"Really? Do I need to ask with whom?"

"Nathan," Marcy unnecessarily replied, closing her eyes as visions of him danced through her mind.

"So things are going well between you two?"

"Very well." She paused before admitting, "Natasha, he's everything I want."

"Then don't let him go," Natasha advised.

"I don't plan on it," Marcy promised.

"Good."

"I'm sorry," Marcy apologized. "Here I am going on and on and you called me."

"Don't be silly," Natasha lightly admonished. "Damien

and I just wanted to invite you and Nathan to dinner to-night."

"I'd love it. Do you want me to ask Nathan?"

"No, I'll call him. How does 7:30 at Thalia sound?"

"Fine," Marcy agreed. "Thanks for the invite."

"You're welcome, and Marcy?"

"Yes."

"Thank you for caring about my brother. I have the feeling he needs you," Natasha foretold.

"I need him." She paused before confessing, "I love him, Natasha." She had to tell someone before she burst.

"I know," Natasha happily whispered. "We'll see you two tonight, and we'll work on getting that brother of mine to open up," Natasha promised.

"That sounds like a plan. See you and Dami tonight," Marcy echoed as she hung up.

About twenty minutes later, her phone rang again. She was deep in thought and started to ignore it, clicking keys on her computer furiously as a new strategy began forming in her mind.

"Marcy Johnson," she absently responded.

"Hi, beautiful."

She immediately stopped typing and sighed. "Hi, what are you doing?" She reclined in her chair, and caressing the phone in her hands, she wished it were Nathan's handsome face instead.

"Thinking about you." Her heart flipped in her chest.

"Oh" was all she could manage, and he laughed softly.

"Were you thinking about me?"

"Always."

"Good," he approved. "Did Tash call you about dinner?"

"Yes, she did."

"Can I pick you up?" he offered.

"You'd better," she threatened. He laughed, and she

closed her eyes, savoring the sound. She could feel his warm breath moving over her yearning skin—her face, neck, shoulders and breasts.

"Around seven?"

She pondered his question. Natasha had set dinner for 7:30.

"Make it six," she suggested.

"What are we going to do with the extra time?" he drawled.

"We'll think of something," she assured, visualizing something very appealing.

"I'm already thinking of something." His roguishly spoken words had her breath catching in her throat. "I miss you." Her audible sigh caressed him. He could see her, feel her and taste her.

"I miss you, too. I wish you were here now."

"So do I," he groaned.

"We can survive for a few more hours."

"Eight long hours to be exact." He sighed.

"Did you have to tell me that?" she echoed his previous groan.

"Sorry," he hopefully suggested. "We could meet for lunch."

She was sorely tempted, but one glance at her cluttered desk made her refuse.

"I'd love to, but I'm swamped with work," she regretfully declined. "Daddy's going to fire me if I don't start taking care of business."

"I doubt that, but I understand." Nathan sighed again. "I'll see you tonight, then."

"I can't wait."

"Me neither. Bye, baby."

"Bye," she echoed as they reluctantly rang off.

She placed a hand on her heart, willing it to slow its

rapid pace. He missed her. He couldn't wait to see her again. She wished she had taken him up on lunch, but she knew she had made the right choice; she had a lot of work to do. Besides, they said absence made the heart grow fonder!

Refocusing on her computer, she tried to force her thoughts away from the man she loved and back on work. The man she loved—what wonderful words those were. The only thing better would be to hear him admit that he was in love with her, too.

Chapter 11

"Nathan, stop it," Marcy seriously scolded as his hands continued to pull the dress off her shoulders.

"Stop what?" His eyes danced mischievously as he gently bit into her bare shoulder, sending shivers down her spine.

"We're going to be late," she insisted, pulling his hands from her waist and turning to face him. "Don't you dare kiss me again," she warned. This was the third time she had repaired her lipstick.

He ignored her and pressed his mouth to hers. Her hands rested on his shoulder before twining around his neck as she kissed him back. Their tongues engaged in a tantalizing game of hide-and-seek. As his hands moved to her back and pulled the zipper of her dress farther down, she pressed against his shoulders until he released her lips.

"What?" He faked innocence as his lips settled in the crook of her neck.

"Nathan, it's after seven." She fought him and herself. "We have to go."

"They're newlyweds. Do you really think they're going to be on time?" he rationalized, hands entangling in her hair and pulling her lips back to his.

"Nathan…" Her words were muffled against his lips. Lord, he could kiss!

"I love your mouth. It's so soft and sweet and…" He lowered his lips toward hers again, but she avoided him.

"Baby, we've already done this." She glanced at the rumpled bed before returning to stare into his dark, dangerous eyes. "Several times."

"Practice makes perfect," he argued, nibbling at her lips.

"We're already perfect together," she said and sighed as his tongue touched hers.

"Mmm, show me how perfect we are," he invited as his mouth ravaged. His hand caressed her bare back.

"Later, baby, later," Marcy promised, using every ounce of strength she possessed to push out of his arms and reposition her dress on her shoulders before trying to refasten it.

"Here, let me help you," he offered, walking behind her.

"Help me put it back on, not take it off," she chided.

"Oh, all right," he grudgingly obliged, sliding the zipper up and releasing her.

"You are terrible." She smiled as he kissed her palm.

"But you want me—" his eyes sparkled "—don't you?"

"Very much," she agreed, retrieving her hand and turning to face the mirror to fix her lipstick for the fourth time. "But now we have to go," she firmly responded, turning from the mirror to face him.

"If you insist," he acquiesced with a sigh. *Why did they have to have dinner with anyone tonight? He would settle for just having her for his appetizer, main course and dessert.*

"I do." Despite her resolve, she leaned toward him for a kiss, but then suddenly pulled back knowing it wouldn't end with a mere kiss.

He smiled at her and held out her coat, which she slipped into. He kissed her cheek before opening the door and following her out.

"I'll be good for now, but later, I'm going to be very bad," he promised as they stepped into the elevator.

"How bad?" she thoughtfully asked.

"Very." He nearly growled the promise, walking determinedly toward her as the doors closed.

"I'm sorry we're late," Marcy apologized to Damien and Natasha when she and Nathan entered the restaurant around 7:45 and were shown to their table.

"No problem. We just got here ourselves." Damien's eyes narrowed when Nathan sat down close to his sister, familiarly draping his arm across the back of her chair.

"Good." Marcy smiled up at Nathan before refocusing her gaze on her brother and his wife.

"What kept you two?" Natasha smiled knowingly, and Marcy steeled herself not to blush.

"I was having some trouble with my...zipper," she truthfully responded and glared at Nathan as he chuckled softly.

"Ah, I see," Natasha responded, glancing happily at the two of them before turning her eyes to encounter the jaw-clenched profile of her husband. She placed her hand over his, and his face relaxed somewhat as he kissed her cheek.

"So what have you two been up to?" Marcy asked and as everyone laughed held up a hand. "Strike that!"

Nathan ran his fingers down Marcy's bare arm and then back up again. He felt her shudder and pulled her closer. Damien's eyes narrowed as he studied the overt intimacy between the two.

Feeling her husband's tension, Natasha decided it was the perfect time to make their announcement. "You're probably wondering why Damien and I invited you to dinner tonight."

"We thought you just missed us." Nathan tore his eyes away from Marcy to smile at his sister.

"True, but there's another reason." Natasha beamed.

Marcy noticed for the first time that she was positively radiant. She wondered…

"Natasha, are you…?" Marcy stopped herself, not wanting to finish that sentence in case she was wrong.

"Am I what?" Natasha's smile brightened.

"Dami?" Marcy glanced at his ecstatic face and knew what she was thinking was correct.

"We're going to have a baby," he confirmed for her.

"That's wonderful!" Marcy was out of her chair and hugging them both.

"Congratulations." Nathan shook Damien's hand and kissed his sister's cheek.

"Have you told the grandparents?" Marcy asked as she resumed her seat, sitting on the edge leaning toward the happy couple.

"Yes, earlier today. They've already named the baby, decided what school he or she will attend and what his or her career will be." Natasha smiled tolerantly.

"Yes, they would." Marcy laughed.

"I'm happy for you both," Nathan responded. He could see her as a mother with Damien beside her as if he had always been there and always would be—just as he could see Marcy always beside him.

"Thank you." Natasha smiled at him through happy tears. "Oh, I need to go and fix my face."

"I'll go with you." Marcy grabbed her hand as they walked away laughing and crying excitedly.

"Women." Damien smiled lovingly as they left.

"They are a necessary evil," Nathan agreed.

"Yes, they are," Damien agreed and lost the battle he had been waging with himself since Nathan and Marcy had arrived. "So, Nathan, what's going on between you and my sister?"

"Damien, I know you're worried about Marcy, but she's a grown woman, not a child. I think she can handle her affairs very well on her own," Nathan coolly replied. He wasn't going to discuss his feelings or relationship with Marcy with her brother.

"How not so subtly you tell me to butt out." Damien smiled despite himself. He liked him. If he could only shake this feeling that he was hiding something— something that was going to end up hurting Marcy.

"I wouldn't use those words, but since you did, yes," Nathan agreed.

"I don't want my sister hurt. Surely you can understand that." Though his face had relaxed somewhat, his tone was still hard and unbending.

"Of course I can. It's not my intention to hurt her." Nathan met his intense eyes without flinching.

"The road to hell is paved miles deep with good intentions," Damien coolly reminded.

"I know," Nathan agreed. He more than anyone knew that only too well.

"What are you into?" Damien's candor obviously surprised Nathan.

"Nothing illegal, I assure you."

"That's a relief—somewhat." Damien continued to stare at him with piercing eyes and received a purposefully noncommittal gaze in response. "I have this feeling that I just can't shake.

"What's that?"

"That you're hiding something."

Nathan shrugged. "I'm not."

The two men stared at each other intensely. Nathan appeared truthful, but Damien wasn't buying it. He didn't quite trust him, and that was a problem since he and his sister were now romantically involved.

"You're lying," Damien bluntly accused.

When Natasha and Marcy return from the powder room, they sensed tension. Their men were silently staring at each other intensely.

"Dami, I hope you didn't do what I think you did," Marcy warned.

"That depends on what you think I did," he coolly replied as Natasha resumed her seat beside him.

"Dammit, Damien, you already played the big brother scene at the rehearsal dinner," Marcy hissed as she sat down beside Nathan. "Now you need to back off!"

Natasha covered Damien's hand with hers when he opened his mouth to angrily respond. "We are not going to have an argument in public, so you two will stop this right now," she softly yet firmly ordered.

They knew she meant business. Though he wanted to pursue this, Damien didn't want to upset his pregnant wife; neither did Marcy. Therefore, they acquiesced and remained silent.

"That's better." Natasha smiled, satisfied.

"I'm sorry, Natasha, but I've lost my appetite." Marcy suddenly stood. "Nathan, will you take me home?"

"Of course." He also stood and possessively took her hand.

"Marcy, don't leave," Natasha implored.

"I think it's for the best, Damien, and I will simply glare at each other all evening if I stay," she predicted. "You have wonderful news to celebrate. Have a nice dinner."

She kissed Natasha's cheek, totally ignored her brother and preceded Nathan on the way out.

"Damien Johnson…" Natasha turned angry eyes on him.

"He's sleeping with her," he tersely accused in his defense as he watched them walk away.

"That's their business," Natasha calmly replied. "Did you say that to him?"

"No, all I said was—" He began to defend himself, but she held up a hand forestalling him.

"I can imagine what you did say. I also understand your concerns," she admitted.

"You do?"

"Yes, but you were wrong to interfere. It's Marcy's life, and she has the right to make her own decisions." She gently kissed his stiff cheek.

"She's my sister," he stated, as if that justified everything. She smiled at him tolerantly.

"And he's my brother, but I respect his privacy—just as you need to respect Marcy's."

His jaw clenched. "He's hiding something."

"Maybe, but it's not up to you to find out what it is."

"Natasha, I can't—"

"Babe, Marcy's a grown woman—a grown furious woman," she corrected.

He sighed. "I know. Are you angry with me, too?"

"No, I love you more than I could ever be angry with you." She kissed his lips.

"I'm sorry about ruining your dinner party," he apologized, arm going around her shoulders pulling her close.

"It's never a hardship spending an evening alone with you." She touched his cheek gently. "You don't have to apologize to me, but perhaps you should to Marcy," she suggested.

"She's not going to make it easy," he predicted.

"Serves you right."

"You're supposed to be on my side." He tweaked her nose playfully.

"I am," she promised. "In fact, I know two people you can worry about all you want." She placed his hand on her flat stomach, and his face relaxed.

"I think I can handle that very well," he promised as he kissed her. "I love you both."

"We love you, too," she reciprocated. "Now feed us. We're starving," she ordered, and he laughed as she intended.

"Marcy it's okay. Damien was just doing what any big brother would do." Nathan tried to calm her down as she angrily paced in her apartment.

"How can you defend his deplorable behavior?" She turned furious eyes in his direction.

"Because I understand it." Nathan grabbed her shoulders to keep her still. "So do you."

"What are you hiding, Nathan?"

Her question surprised him. As if burned, he released her shoulders and turned away from her.

"You said you would wait until I could tell you," he reminded.

"I know, and I meant that." At her words, he turned to face her again.

"Then why are you asking me now?" He rubbed his chin, and she smiled.

She walked over and placed her hands on his chest. "Because I'm sure that's what Damien asked you."

"He did."

"What did you tell him?"

"To mind his own business." She placed a hand on his

chin, checking one side of his face carefully and then the other. "What are you looking for?"

"A bruise," she said and chuckled. "You mean he didn't hit you?"

"No—" he smiled slightly "—but I'm sure he wanted to."

"I'm sorry." Her hand cupped his cheek.

"Don't be." He covered her hand with his. "He reacted the way I would have if you were my sister."

"Perish that thought!" She made a distasteful face, and he laughed. "You're not on the run from the law, are you?"

"No." he smiled dryly.

"Then whatever it is, it can't be that bad," she decided.

He wished he could tell her she was right. Instead, he kissed her lips gently and then walked toward the door before he gave into an ever-growing need to confess everything to her about his job, including information regarding his imminent departure—something he knew he couldn't do, but Lord he wanted to be honest with her as she so effortlessly was with him.

"Where are you going?" She placed a staying hand on his arm.

"Home." He smiled as she purposefully shook her head no while pulling him toward the hallway.

"I don't think so." She placed butterfly kisses over his face as they danced into the bedroom.

"What do you have on your mind, Marcy Johnson?" His lips played with hers, all thoughts of leaving forgotten.

"You'll see," she promised, jumping slightly as thunder sounded in the distance and lightning flashed briefly. "There's a storm brewing outside."

"Inside, too," he promised, hands going around her waist, pulling her close.

"Mmm," she whispered against his neck while eager

hands dispensed with his jacket, tie and shirt. "If you left, I'd be worried about you getting home safely."

"We can't have that." Focused hands unzipped her dress and slid it down and off her body to pool at her feet.

"Besides, you promised me you'd be very bad tonight," she reminded.

"And I meant it," he vowed into her mouth.

They quickly stripped off the remainder of each other's clothes and then fell across the bed, limbs entangling and mouths meeting and dancing. He forgot the reasons why he should stay away from her; he forgot everything as her soft body melted invitingly around his.

The freak thunderstorm outside began to rage in concert with the tempest they were creating within each other. Thunder clapped loudly in unison with the thudding of their hearts, and they pressed closer. Lightning flashed, echoing the movement of their hands as they caressed and explored. A sudden torrential downpour of rain pelted against the windowpanes as strong and sudden as the tidal wave of emotions washing over them. The fury of the storm matched their own frenzy as they sought to deny the laws of physics and merge their two bodies into one.

Nathan reclined on his back, and Marcy straddled his hips, hands resting on his muscled chest. Her back arched elegantly as a streak of lightning illuminated the room temporarily. Unable to stand the small distance between them, Nathan's hands pulled her down until she was lying across his chest. They sought to quench the destructive fires blazing brightly inside, threatening to quickly reduce them to spent ashes.

"I love you, Nathan," she whispered, her hair covering their faces when she kissed him lingeringly before he could respond.

At her admission, their feverish pace suddenly changed,

and he loved her slowly, tenderly as if she were the most precious person in the world to him, which indeed she was. They kissed long, slow and deep. Threading his fingers in her hair, Nathan unnecessarily held her mouth against his; she had neither the desire nor the intention of moving away from him not even for a second. As they drank thirstily from each other's mouth, he rolled her beneath him in one fluid movement as their slow dance continued. The simple beauty of their perfect closeness brought tears to her eyes, which he kissed away while his body gently, stroked hers.

She stared into his expressive eyes and learned all she needed to know—everything he didn't say but felt; he loved her, too. She could wait until he was ready to admit it. For now, he let his body and heart tell her what he couldn't yet say, and for now it was enough because she knew without a doubt he would utter the all-important words very soon.

Nathan felt her climax come in a long shuddering release, and still his body continued to caress hers until she took him with her. A deafening clap of thunder sounded— or was it the frantic beating of their pounding hearts? His mouth sought and found hers, and they shared numerous lengthy, earth-shattering kisses that added the final layer of oneness their bodies were seeking.

Her eyes wanted to close, but she kept them partially opened and focused on Nathan until she felt herself sinking, drowning and spiraling toward ultimate pleasure, pulling him along with her until they both found blessed release. He collapsed on her, burying his face in the crook of her neck, and she held him close as their ragged breathing slowly returned to normal. The fury of the storm inside was temporarily spent while the storm outside raged on furiously.

They both knew it had been different this time; this

wasn't simply about physical release. They had willingly given their hearts and souls tonight, and nothing would ever be the same between them again.

The next morning, Marcy and Damien sat across from each other across a small table in the rehearsal hall. She hadn't been surprised to receive his call this morning; they had never been able to stay angry with each other for very long.

"I'm sorry, Marce," he reluctantly apologized and then took a gulp of coffee, as if to wash the bitter words down.

"Say it like you mean it," she softly ordered.

"Don't press your luck."

"Tell Natasha thank you for making you do this." She laughed at his dry tone.

"I will." He didn't bother to deny his wife's hand in his apology. "Maybe you could call her and—"

"Gave you a hard time, did she?" Marcy interrupted him and intuitively smiled at his confirmatory expression. "I don't think I will call her. You deserve to suffer a little."

"You can be so heartless sometimes."

"You deserve it after what you did," she chided.

"Marce, I only said what I did because I love you."

"You don't have to tell me that." She slid her chair until she was sitting close beside him and kissed his cheek. "I love you, too."

"But?" He waited, knowing there was more.

"But I would appreciate it if you would let me handle Nathan. I know what I'm doing."

He doubted that, but then that was just Marcy—jump first and look later. "I'll try to mind my own business," he relented.

"Thank you, Dami." She hugged him close. "I'm happy for you, Daddy," she whispered against his ear.

"Thanks," he said. When he pulled back, he was grinning like an idiot.

"How scared are you?" Marcy asked.

"Terrified," he admitted. "But don't tell Tasha."

"Your secret's safe with me," she promised. Her eyes strayed to the wall clock and she jumped up. "I'm late. I gotta go."

"To see Nathan?"

"No." She smiled at him tolerantly. "I'm seeing him later. Now, I'm off to work."

She waved at him brightly, and he sighed heavily while watching her hurriedly leave. His baby sister was in love, and he wanted to be happy for her, but he was worried instead. He liked Nathan, but he wasn't sure he should trust him, and if he couldn't, Marcy definitely shouldn't. He'd keep his suspicions to himself for Marcy's and Natasha's sake, but he was going to keep a careful eye on the situation. If Nathan looked as though he was going to hurt Marcy, brother-in-law or no brother-in-law, he was going to skin him alive.

Chapter 12

Nathan strolled down the hall to his suite, whistling a happy tune after a wonderful night and morning of loving Marcy, and before opening the door, he sensed something was not right. His smile faded, and he became quiet and lethal as a predatory cat. Someone was here or had been here. Slowly, his hand moved under his jacket and drew out his gun before carefully opening the door. His eyes slowly touched on every corner of the room as he remained silhouetted in the doorway.

"Move and you're dead," he ordered, pointing his gun at the figure standing by the window. "Hands over your head and walk slowly toward me."

The figure complied, and when he came into view, Nathan lowered his gun with a muffled curse. His heart sank because there was only one reason his visitor was here—to let him know it was time to leave for his next mission.

"Nice to see you're still on your toes even though you're on holiday." The man smiled.

"Benson." Nathan replaced his gun and walked into the room, closing the door behind him.

"This is for you." Benson handed him a large envelope with an official seal on it.

"Everything all set?" Nathan took the envelope and threw it carelessly on the bed.

"Nearly." Benson raised an eyebrow at his blasé attitude. "We're waiting on satellite confirmation of the rebel camp, which should come anytime."

"Is the team assembled?" Nathan asked, and for the first time in his life didn't really care.

"Ready and waiting. This is going to be a dangerous, extremely delicate undertaking, Nathan." Benson paused before reminding, "We're invading another country's sovereignty."

"I know," he agreed on a sigh. "We tried diplomatic channels, but the Yemen government refused to cooperate with us. They've left us no choice. Besides, everything suggests they were complicit in our envoy and his aides being taken in the first place. We're better off going it alone."

"True, but you know if you're captured…" Benson's words trailed off ominously.

"We're on our own. The United States will deny having sent us," Nathan unemotionally finished. He had no intention of failing or being captured. They'd be in and out of Yemen before the enemy knew what had hit them.

"It would be so much easier if we could use drones." Benson sighed.

"We might kill the hostages if we did that. The best way is boots on the ground." Nathan scratched his chin before rigidly asking the dreaded question, "How long do I have?"

"A few days, maybe a week, but don't count on it. You'll receive your extraction orders—"

"I know the drill." Nathan snapped the words as he walked over to stare moodily out of the window.

"Anything wrong?" Benson's eyes bore into his back. He was about to be dropped into the mouth of hell; they had to have him in tip-top shape, and he seemed far from that right now.

"No, everything is fine." Nathan turned from the window. "I'm just a little antsy." He remained stone-faced as Benson studied him closely.

"Are you sure?"

"Absolutely."

"Very well, then." Benson frowned but shook his head and walked toward the door. "Oh, and Nathan?"

"Yeah?"

"Enjoy the rest of your time with your family." The man smiled, and then he was gone.

"Yeah." Nathan sighed, pushing his fists into his pockets as he stared moodily out into the bright, sunlit Manhattan skyline, which made the darkness encasing his heart all that more noticeable.

A few days. He had only a few days left. He glanced at the file on his bed and recoiled from opening it as if it were a poisonous snake—it was worse than that, it were the thing that was going to take him away from the woman he loved and he was powerless to stop it. He turned and glared out of the window, fingers rubbing his suddenly aching head.

What was he going to tell Marcy? He couldn't tell her the truth, but he had to tell her something. What? If he told her that he had to leave for work but couldn't tell her where he was going and had no idea when he'd be back, she'd naturally have questions he wouldn't be able to answer. His necessary silence would inevitably lead to righteous anger on her part and they'd argue; he didn't want their last days together to be spent at odds. The alternative was just as distasteful—leaving without saying goodbye, disappearing without a word. He couldn't do that to her. The very thought chilled him to the bone.

Maybe he could… He paused and sighed loudly. Hell, he honestly didn't know what he was going to tell her, but he'd better decide soon, because time was quickly running out.

Miserably, he turned from the window, sat down heavily on the bed and angrily tore open the envelope that was about to destroy his life.

"Marcy, what are you doing here?" Nathan reluctantly stepped aside as the woman who had occupied his thoughts for the past hours entered his hotel room.

"What kind of a greeting is that?" She laughed, kissing his lips briefly before he moved away.

Her eyes followed him as he walked over to the table and picked up a folder and papers before placing them in a manila envelope. With them in his hand, he turned to face her but made no move toward her.

"What's wrong, Nathan?" She threw her jacket over a chair and walked over to him.

"Nothing, I'm just tired."

"I'm tired, too." She wound her arms around his neck and pressed close to his rigid body. "Why don't we rest together?"

"I don't think so." He disentangled himself, walked over and placed the folder in a briefcase, clicking it shut and twirling the brass wheels to lock it. "You should go home."

"What's the matter with you?" She touched his arm, and he slowly turned to face her.

"Nothing." His eyes were devoid of any emotion.

"Nothing?" she disbelievingly echoed. "Try again."

"All right. If you must know, I think we rushed into things without thinking through the consequences." He inwardly groaned as he uttered the lie.

"We need to cool things down." She slowly dropped her hand away from him. "Is that it?"

"Yes, that's it," he distastefully agreed.

He wanted to pull her into his arms and tell her how much he loved her, but he didn't; he couldn't. Instead, he met her penetrating gaze unflinchingly waiting for her angry response, but it never materialized.

"Sorry, Nathan, but I won't be neatly swept under the rug." She startled him by her smile and light, almost playful tone.

"That's not what I'm trying to do," he denied. "I just think we made a mistake."

"We didn't make a mistake, baby," she softly denied.

Where was the anger and outrage? He expected her to rant and rave, maybe try to claw his eyes out but not this calm almost amused tolerance. She never did what he expected, which was one of the things he loved about her.

"Marcy, I don't want..." His voice trailed off—the distasteful words he needed to utter refusing to pass his lips.

"What? What don't you want?" She moved closer to him. "Finish that sentence. I dare you."

"I don't want to hurt you." He sighed.

"Then why are you trying to do just that?"

"I'm not." He rubbed his chin, stopping when she smiled. "I'm trying to save you."

"From what?" She touched his cheek gently. "From you? From us?"

"Yes." He sighed.

"Nathan, I don't even pretend to understand what's going on in here." She touched his head with her fingers.

"But I understand this." She touched his heart and paused before framing his face with her hands. "I love you."

"Marcy, don't." He couldn't bear to hear her admit that again. Hearing it last night had been hard enough.

"I can't help it. I do love you," she reiterated, pulling his lips down to hers. "I'm so in love with you," she vowed.

"Marcy…"

"I love you, Nathan," she softly yet urgently interrupted him.

This woman held his heart. He would do anything for her, which is why it killed him not to be able to tell her the truth about his impending departure, but he could tell her how he felt about her. It was eating him alive to keep it to himself.

"I love you, too," he admitted against her lips.

"What?" Her heart stopped beating at his admission and she pulled back slightly to smile at him.

"I love you," he repeated.

"You do?" She couldn't believe this was finally happening.

"You know I do," he gently countered. She did, but she couldn't believe he had finally admitted it. "I love you with all my heart," he echoed, sealing the vow with a deep kiss.

"Why are you telling me now, when a few seconds ago you were trying to push me away?"

"Are you complaining?" Despite himself, he smiled before encircling her waist with his arms.

"No, not at all," she quickly denied. "I'm just…overwhelmed."

"That's how I feel about you," he sympathized. "I didn't want this to happen, but I realize now I couldn't stop it."

"No," she softly agreed. "Make love with me," she offered, taking his hand and pulling him over to the bed.

"Nothing would please me more." He began unbuttoning her blouse, and then they slowly divested each other of their clothes.

He drew her to him gently yet firmly. Their bodies melted together, engaging in their own private seduction. Their hands and lips savored the different textures and flavors while they lost and found themselves. It was special, complete, without comparison; they gave each other all that they had—surrendered everything without regret or remorse.

Soft sighs and murmurs gave way to deep groans and whimpers as they gave themselves over to love. It was as if they had never made love before. It was different this time—perfect because each had confessed their love. As they sighed into each other's mouths, Marcy doubted if anything would ever be this perfect again.

"I don't want to hurt you, Marcy," Nathan whispered against her temple much later when they were still.

"You won't. You couldn't." She snuggled closer to him. "Tell me again," she softly ordered.

He easily complied. "I love you, Marcy Johnson."

"Nothing will ever come between us," she sleepily whispered against his chest.

"No, nothing," he sadly agreed.

He pulled her close and wished her words were true. However, he knew that all too soon his duty would rear its ugly head, and then he was going to hurt her more than anyone ever had and he was utterly helpless to stop it—just as he had been powerless against falling headlong, hopelessly in love with her.

Nathan had spent every second of the past four days with Marcy. He'd tried to tell and show her how much he loved her; praying that would get her through the pain his unexplained absence was going to cause when he was forced to leave her.

Inevitably, this morning, he had received the activation he had been dreading. It was now his last day with the love of his life, and he was determined it would be a happy one. He sat with her now in floor seats at a New York game. He watched every movement she made, listened to every word she uttered, no matter how small. He didn't want to miss a second of this, their last day together—for a while.

She caught him glancing at her several times with an unreadable and almost sad expression. "What's wrong, baby?"

"Nothing, I'm just floored by how much I love you," he seriously replied.

"Now you tell me, when we're surrounded by thousands of strangers," she whispered in his ear.

"I'll tell you later when we're alone," he promised, and despite the loud noise, throngs of people and constant action on the court a few feet away, he kissed her lingeringly.

"What was that for?" She sighed as his lips left hers.

"Because I wanted to." He forced himself to smile as he picked up her soda and took a big gulp.

"Are you sure nothing's wrong?" she persisted, unable to shake the feeling that all was not well with him.

"Everything is great," he insisted, pulling her close as they continued watching the game.

Despite his denials, she knew he was bothered and wished he would let her help him through it, whatever it was. He seemed to desperately need this—need to be here with her now; therefore, she relented and bit back the questions threatening to spill from her lips.

He would tell her what was wrong when he was ready, and she would listen and be there for him—always. She pushed her worries aside and snuggled closer to the man she loved who loved her back.

"What's next?" she asked as they left Madison Square Garden hours later.

"I thought I'd take you back to my hotel room." He placed an arm around her shoulders and pulled her close.

She smiled up at him, "Then what?"

"I'll order up some champagne."

"Go on," she prompted.

"Then I plan to spend the entire night reexploring every centimeter of your delicious body." He stopped and kissed her in the middle of the full parking lot. "With my hands and mouth."

"Oh, yes. I like the way you think." She groaned at the blatant desire written in his eyes.

He traced her lips with his tongue, "So are you game for some one-on-one action with me?"

"Oh, baby, you know I am," she promised and they laughingly ran toward the car.

Nathan quietly walked over to where Marcy lay curled up on his side of the bed—where he had lain only minutes earlier.

She stirred sleepily and half opened her eyes when he bent down to kiss her tenderly. "Go back to sleep, baby," he whispered.

"Nathan…love you," she whispered, eyes closing heavily.

"I love you, too, Marcy, very much. Remember that," he whispered, kissing her forehead softly before straightening.

"Come back to bed," she invited in hushed tones, her eyes still closed.

"I will in a minute. I have to make a phone call." The

words almost choked him because they were a lie. He gently pushed her hair away from her beautiful face, and she smiled slightly before drifting back off into sleep.

He felt as if his heart was literally being ripped from his body and even though he had come to a long overdue decision to leave Black Ops after this mission, even though he knew this was the last time he would ever have to leave her like this, it was still killing him. But for now—right now—he had to disappear from her life. There was no other choice possible.

The hardest thing he ever did was turn away from her and walk out the door knowing when she woke the knowledge that he was gone would destroy her—knowing there was absolutely nothing he could do except keep right on walking away from her.

Several hours later, Marcy stretched luxuriously and wondered why she didn't encounter Nathan's solid form. Opening drowsy eyes and squinting against the bright morning sun, she turned in Nathan's direction, but he wasn't there.

"Nathan?" She sat up in bed. Where was he? "Nathan?"

She vaguely remembered waking up in the middle of the night to find him standing over her. Had he been dressed? She couldn't remember. Maybe he had gone downstairs for something. Her hand reached across on the pillow and encountered her phone sitting on top of a crisp piece of paper on which was written, *Play me.*

What was that man up to? Chuckling, she turned on her phone and saw she had a new voice recording. Pressing Play, she waited for it to begin.

"Hi, baby." She smiled as Nathan's voice filtered across the speaker, but that smile quickly faded as the message continued. *"I'm so sorry, but I had to leave like this be-*

cause if I didn't you would have asked questions I couldn't answer, and I didn't want to leave with angry words between us. I have to leave because of my job, but I can't tell you why or where I have to go. Just know that I'll take you with me in my heart. When I'm able, I'll come back to you, and I'll explain everything. I promise. I love you, baby."

Her mouth dropped open in shock, and she replayed the message again and again and again. Nathan was gone? This couldn't be happening. Last night, he had told her he loved her—had meant it with everything he was. They had shared a beautiful, wonderful time together. Only now did she realize he had been saying goodbye to her.

"Nathan!" She jumped out of bed and ran through the entire suite looking for him but to no avail.

A few minutes later, she sank back down onto the bed after finding his clothes and other possessions gone. What the hell was going on? Nathan had loved her, had made her feel as if she was his life, and now he was gone. He had left her without paying her the courtesy of saying goodbye to her face-to-face, without letting her know where he was going or for how long, without a thought for the pain his leaving would cause her? How could he do this to her? How could he?

Her hand crumpled the paper until it was a small wad and flung her phone across the room sending it crashing into a wall with a loud crack before it splintered like her broken heart. Despite promising herself she wouldn't, tears of anger and pain began falling heedlessly down her face.

She fell back against the pillows on which Nathan had lain with her a short while ago, curled against it and wept bitterly.

She didn't go into work that day; she didn't know how she made it home. She had spent the entire day where she was now, sitting on her sofa, staring unseeingly out of the living room window, trying to comprehend what had happened and why Nathan had willfully broken her heart.

She had forgotten she and Nathan's dinner plans with Damien and Natasha until Natasha had called to remind her a little while ago. She'd told her she couldn't make it and had hung up before Natasha could say anything else or before she could place Dami on the phone. She didn't want to face anyone yet. She needed some time for her heart to assimilate what her mind already had—that Nathan was gone and he had taken her heart with him.

She sat on her sofa in the dark, knees curled up to her chest, feeling completely empty; she supposed it was better than the pain that had threatened to consume her all day long. The doorbell rang several times before she registered the sound, which was quickly followed by Damien beating on the door and yelling her name. Oh, God. How long had he been here?

"I'm coming," she yelled, knowing he wouldn't go away until she answered. She switched on a light on the way to open the door, partially illuminating the dark room.

One look at her sad features and Damien took her into his arms. "What's wrong?"

"Nathan is gone," she whispered.

She had promised herself she wasn't going to cry again, but it was a hard vow to keep feeling her brother's comforting arms go around her and hearing his softly sworn curse at her news.

"What do you mean he's gone?" He pulled her into her apartment with one arm around her shoulders; his other hand grasped Natasha's, who followed him inside.

She shrugged miserably. "He left without a word last night."

"What?" The single word was spoken with quiet fury.

"Why would he do that?" Natasha grabbed Marcy's free hand.

"I don't know, and I don't care," Marcy harshly responded and then could have kicked herself as she noticed the sadness that crossed Natasha's face at her words.

"When I find him, I'm going to beat him to a pulp," Damien quietly promised before he could stop himself.

"Dami." Marcy shook her head slightly before glancing toward Natasha.

He swore softly. "I'm sorry, Tasha," he pulled Natasha close and kissed her hair.

"No, you don't have to apologize." Natasha's arm went around his waist. Then to Marcy she said, "I don't understand why Nathan would do this."

"I don't care what his reasons are. He's not going to get away with this!" The outburst came out before Damien could stop it.

"Dami, I want you to promise me you will stay out of this," Marcy pleaded. "If anyone is going to do physical harm to Nathan when he returns, it's going to be me," she promised in dead earnest.

"Marcy—"

"No. I mean it. Promise you won't interfere."

"I don't know why I worry about you," he joked, hoping she wouldn't notice he wasn't promising her any such thing.

"You can worry about me all you want, but I don't need you to fight my battles." She gave him a tearful smile. "It is nice to know you're in my corner, though."

"Always." He hugged her close. Despite her brave words, he felt his sister's arm tighten around him, and his tightened in response. She was in pain, but she didn't want to let it show. When he saw Nathan Carter again, he was going to slowly, methodically kill him!

* * *

Dressed in tan fatigues, Nathan made his way through the treacherous mountains of Yemen. His mind should have been on detecting booby traps, running into enemy interference or a host of other possible threats to him and his men, but instead it was filled with thoughts of Marcy.

He had been gone two weeks—two miserably long weeks that had seemed like years. He wondered what she was doing. Was she sitting in her office pretending to work, trying to hide the pain he had inflicted upon her? Was she wishing him dead or damning him to hell? Whatever she thought and felt about him he knew was justified.

He prayed she would forgive him, prayed this mission would be over with soon so that he could return to her; he was doing everything in his power to make that happen quickly. Without trying, he could see her beautiful face smiling at him. He could hear her infectious laughter and smell her exotic perfume mixing lethally with her own unique scent. He felt her…

"Sir? Sir!" A voice forcefully yet quietly brought him out of his revelry.

"What?" he quietly snapped, turning cold eyes on the younger man.

"I know you're in charge, but all of our lives are in your hands," a man bluntly replied. Nathan bristled at the polite rebuke.

"I'm aware of that!" he snapped.

"You've been distracted for quite a while, sir." The other man forced himself to continue. He knew he was bordering on insubordination, but all of their lives were in Carter's hands; he had to be focused, something he hadn't been since beginning this deployment.

"If I want your opinion, Smith, I'll give it to you," Nathan angrily rebuked. "Now cut the chatter. We're almost there," he ordered and then sent hand signals to the members of his squadron.

Smith was right. His mind wasn't on his job, and that could lead to deaths. He instinctively knew this was how it would be every time he left Marcy if he stayed with the unit, and sooner or later, he would be responsible for someone dying; he wouldn't let that happen.

His decision to leave the unit was the right one for everyone concerned, but for now he had to concentrate on getting the hostages, his men and himself out of this hellhole in one piece. Then he was going home to his life—to Marcy.

Chapter 13

February was drawing to a close. Marcy sat behind her desk at work staring hollowly out of the windows that made up her back wall. A month—a whole month—had passed and she hadn't received a single word from Nathan—not a text, a phone message or a hurriedly scribbled note. Nothing! The State Department refused to give her any information when she had called simply saying he was out of the country on business and couldn't be reached, as if she didn't know that already!

With each day that passed, her anger had increased to the point of pure rage. When she saw him again, it would not be a pretty reunion. There was no excuse for his behavior, and she would tell him that along with a few other choice truths if he bothered to show his face.

The buzzer sounded on her desk; she swiveled in her chair and punched a button before snapping, "What is it?"

"Ms. Johnson, there's a man here to see... Sir, excuse me you can't go in there!"

"Marie?" Marcy spoke into the phone before getting up and walking determinedly to the door seconds before it burst open admitting Nathan.

"I can handle this annoyance, Marie. Thank you. She dismissed her assistant, who was covering for Peggy at the front desk, without taking her angry eyes from Nathan's determined face. Dressed all in black, he looked danger-ous and so handsome. She was torn between giving him the tongue lashing he richly deserved and kissing him madly. She wanted to rush into his arms, feel him hold-ing her close and press her starving lips to his, but her feet remained rooted in place. Despite the agony he had put her through, she was ecstatic to see him, but she wouldn't tell him that!

"Marcy." He walked toward her, stopping when her eyebrow rose angrily.

"Nathan," she frigidly rejoined, "what brings you here?"

"Come on, Marcy." He sighed at her flippant tone. "Let me explain."

"Don't you think the time for explanations was a month ago before you left me sleeping snug in your bed and snuck out of town like a coward?" she coldly asked.

"I know you're angry..." he began, rubbing his chin. Another time she would have laughed at the gesture, but not now.

"Angry? Honey, there's not a word for what I am," she assured, placing her hands on her slender hips.

"Come with me so we can talk privately." He reached for her hand, and she wasn't quick enough to avoid him.

"Let go!" she snapped, angrier at herself than him for the elevation of her pulse at his touch.

"Not until you listen to me," he refused, grip tightening on her fingers.

"If you don't unhand me and get out of my office, I'm going to call security," she seriously warned.

His mouth set into unbending lines. They stared each other long and hard, each intent on having their way. He gave in first, expression softening while he gazed lovingly into her turbulent eyes.

"Marcy." He sighed and loosened his hold on her hand. "I know you're angry, and you have every right to be."

"Gee, thanks for your permission to be upset!" Taking advantage of his relaxed grip, she yanked her fingers from his and brushed past him, out of her office. "Marie, call security," she ordered.

"I wouldn't," Nathan quietly suggested to Marie as he followed Marcy into the lobby before refocusing his attention on the woman he loved. "I'm not leaving until we talk."

"Listen you." Marcy poked his muscled chest with her finger. "The time for talking was a month ago. I don't have anything to say to you now!"

"Fine." He took hold of her hand again. "You can listen then because I have plenty to say to you."

"I don't want to hear it, Nathan!" She pulled against his grip. "Too little, too late!"

All he wanted was to pull her into his arms and kiss her endlessly, but he knew that wasn't a good idea at the moment. He had to explain himself, and he was determined to persuade her to give him the chance to.

"I'm not going anywhere until we talk, Marcy." He purposefully kept his voice calm; there was no sense in both of them shouting.

"You had your chance to talk before you left," she angrily reminded. "Oh, that's right," she sarcastically said and smiled. "You were too busy sneaking out of town while I slept in your bed to even say goodbye in person!"

"I left you a note," he quietly reminded her.

"Yes, you did leave me a nice little antiseptic, uninformative message, didn't you?" Her voice rose perceptibly. His touch burned, and her insane need to forget her anger and fall into his arms only incensed her further. "Let go of my hand, Nathan!"

"No," he stubbornly refused.

"Nathan—"

"What's going on out here?" Michael demanded, exiting his office to see what was wrong with his visibly upset daughter.

"Daddy, tell him to let me go," Marcy pleaded.

"Listen here, young man..." Michael's voice faded away when Nathan turned to face him. "Oh, Nathan, it's you."

"Yes, sir." Nathan offered his free hand.

"Well, you have a lot of explaining to do, son," Michael sternly replied after shaking his hand.

"Yes, sir. I realize that," Nathan agreed. "That's what I'm trying to do now, but your daughter's not making it easy." He smiled at Marcy's angry glance. "Has she always been so stubborn?"

"Always." Michael chuckled. "I could tell you stories..."

"Daddy, don't you dare tell him anything!" Marcy placed her free hand on her hip indignantly.

"Give him a chance to explain, baby," Michael suggested. "You know you missed him."

"Oh, Daddy," Marcy groaned in mortification.

"See what he has to say for himself." Michael patted her cheek and then winked at Nathan. "You'd better make it good, son."

"I'll try, sir." Nathan smiled as Michael turned and walked back to his office.

At the door, he turned and smiled. "Nice to have you home, son."

"Thank you, sir."

"Nathan, let go of my hand," Marcy demanded, quietly this time, now aware of Marie doing her best not to stare at them.

"If I do, will you promise to listen to me?"

"Yes," she said and sighed. "I promise."

He eyed her suspiciously. "Cross your heart?"

Despite her anger, she fought a smile. "Cross my heart."

"All right." He released her, half expecting her to bolt, but she didn't.

"I'm listening. Go ahead and talk." She brushed a strand of hair away from her angry but no longer livid face.

"Not here." He glanced at the curious Marie and her father's closed door before taking her hand in his again and guiding her toward the elevator. "Let's get out of here."

She pulled against his hand. "What's wrong with my office?"

"We need to talk privately without interruptions." He punched the button to summon the elevator, and when it arrived, he beckoned her inside.

"Maybe I don't want to go anywhere with you." She stood her ground. "Did you ever think of that?"

"Baby." He stood half in, half out of the elevator bracing the doors open with his shoulder. "I know I hurt you by disappearing the way I did, but I did leave you a message and told you I'd be back," he reminded. "Now I'm here, and I'm not going anywhere. I promise. Just give me a chance to explain, Marcy." He touched her cheek gently. "That's all I'm asking." At her continued silence, he added for good measure, "Please."

Her eyes softened at his plea and gentle touch. Damn him and damn herself for missing him so much. How could she refuse such a sincere request? Yes, she was angry and hurt, but she deserved some answers, and after all they had been to each other, he deserved a chance to explain himself, didn't he?

"All right." She sighed in resignation. "We can go to your hotel—but only to talk."

He smiled at her. "I haven't checked into a hotel yet. I came straight here from the airport. Let's go to your place."

Her frown softened at his admission. Well, it was a point in his favor that seeing her had been his first priority. Bit by bit he was chipping away at her anger.

"We can go to my place on one condition," she decided.

"What's that?"

"When I tell you to leave, you leave."

"I'll agree to your condition if you'll agree to mine," he countered, smiling.

An arched eyebrow rose. "Which is what?"

"You promise to give me five uninterrupted minutes to explain."

"Fine." She agreed after mulling it over for several seconds, and finally walked into the elevator. "Marie, I'll be gone for the rest of the day," she informed her assistant as the doors closed.

Once outside, Nathan led her to the cab he had asked to wait for him. They got in, and he sighed audibly when she placed his carry-on between them and sat as close to her door and as far away from him as she could get. Though she glanced at him briefly, she didn't say a word, and he respected her space. He knew he had a lot to make up for. The important thing was that they were together now, and he had no intention of ever being apart from her again.

When the cab stopped a short while later, Nathan got out and offered her his hand, which she took after a slight hesitation but quickly dropped once out of the cab and walked ahead of him toward her building. Sighing, he retrieved his bag and followed her.

"Good afternoon, Ms. Johnson," Chuck, the doorman, greeted them. "Hi, Mr. Carter, we haven't seen you around here for a while."

"I've been out of the country." Nathan's response received a snort from Marcy.

"Pleasure?"

"Business." Nathan stressed the single word for Marcy's benefit.

"Are you coming or not?" Marcy huffed, glancing over her shoulder. It irked her that everybody was happy he was back home—including herself, she grudgingly admitted.

"She can't wait to get me alone." Nathan winked at the doorman.

"I can, too!" she interjected and bristled as the two men laughed.

"Actually, I'm in trouble," Nathan confided in Chuck. "We're having a lover's spat."

"I know how those can be." Chuck shook his head in sympathy, opening the door for them. "Well, good luck."

"Thanks, I think I need it." Nathan followed Marcy into the building.

After another silent elevator ride, they reached Marcy's apartment and went inside. Nathan smiled as she tossed hair over her shoulder and turned to face him. He carelessly dropped his bag by the door and allowed himself a few seconds to feast his starving eyes on her. The black-and-white skirt suit she wore hugged her curves in all the right places, and her black pumps accentuated every lovely inch of her gorgeous long legs. God, she was beautiful! He wanted to lose himself in her and make them both forget the past month apart had ever happened.

"Stop looking at me like that," she whispered, and his smiling eyes rose to meet her guarded ones.

"Like what?" he innocently asked.

"You know," she softly accused, willing her heart to still its frantic beating. "We didn't come here for *that*."

"For what?" His roguish smile cajoled a tiny one from her, which he delighted in witnessing. Emboldened, he grasped her hand and urged her toward him.

"Nathan—" she fought the insane urge to pull his mouth down to hers and instead pointed to the mantel clock "—your five minutes has started."

"You are so beautiful."

"Nathan…" Her voice hitched at his hungry expression.

"You are." His free hand brushed her hair behind her back. "I'm just stating a well-known fact, ma'am."

"Talk." She was unsuccessful in suppressing a half smile.

"I saw that." His pleased assertion coaxed a broader smile from her. "It's insane how much I missed you—your smile, your touch, your scent."

"It was your own fault," she softly reminded.

"I know," he agreed, cupping her cheek, encouraged when she didn't move away. "I've dreamed about you every day for the past month. I counted the seconds until I could see and touch you again." His thumb caressed her cheek, and he nearly groaned aloud at the simple pleasure. "Didn't you think about me? Didn't you miss me—just a little bit?"

"Maybe." Her noncommittal response elicited a chuckle from him.

"Oh, Marcy." His hand snaked behind her head pulling her closer. "I love you. You know that, don't you?"

"I thought you did." *Remember you're mad at him!* Oh, but that was so hard to do when he was looking at her with such adoration and his touch unleashed a million fluttering butterflies in her stomach.

"You know *I do*," he firmly corrected, fingers caressing the back of her neck.

"Then why...?" She briefly closed her eyes and sighed before continuing, "Why did you leave?"

"I'll explain," he promised, and she nodded in agreement.

Unable to resist any longer, he slowly lowered his mouth to hers, giving her the chance to pull away, but she didn't; instead, she met him halfway. When their lips touched, they both groaned. Their lips teased in butterfly kisses for a few seconds before both having had enough sought out longer contact.

It was a thorough, searing, yet tender kiss. They drank from each other's mouths incessantly, and when he tried to end contact, she placed a hand behind his head and fused his mouth back to hers. She felt him smile against her lips before feasting from her delicious mouth until they were both breathless.

"I missed you so much, Nathan." She sighed against his mouth, pressing closer.

"Missed you more," he responded around nibbles at her moist lips, saying a silent prayer of thanks when she took his hands and pulled him toward the bedroom. "I only have five minutes to explain myself, remember?"

"Oh, and you *will* explain yourself," she said and laughed softly. "I'll give you some extra time."

Once they reached the bedroom, her hands went to work on removing his leather jacket and T-shirt, tossing them onto the immaculate floor before pushing him onto the bed. She smiled down at him as he lay on his back grinning up at her.

"So—" his smile widened when she shrugged out of her jacket and blouse "—do you want to know why I left now?"

"Not at this moment." Her skirt joined her jacket and blouse, and she straddled his hips, lowering her mouth to his. "Let's discuss it later. Okay?"

"Okay," he agreed, meeting her lips halfway in a greedy kiss.

When they were this close, she couldn't think of anything except how much she loved and wanted him. She'd find out why he'd left, but now she intended to celebrate his return. Together, they divested themselves of the scant remainder of her clothes ending with her satin bra—the final barrier between their bare skin and roving hands as they reacquainted themselves with the too long denied pleasure of being this close.

"I love you, Marcy," he whispered against her lips. "I love you so much," he urgently repeated around a groan and rolled her beneath him and slipped into her waiting warmth, which he had longed for every agonizing second he had been away from her.

"I love you, too." She sighed in ecstasy, running her hands down his bare back.

She arched up and took him deeper. She felt alive again, and despite the pain he had caused her, she was still his— mind, body and soul—just as he was still hers.

His mouth caressed hers, engaging in a dance of exquisite passion with hers. His lips and tongue savored as his body devastated. She wrapped slender long limbs around him and forgot everything except the fact that she loved him and always would. He had hurt her terribly, but now he made up for every ounce of pain he had inflicted upon her—giving her pleasure beyond compare—successfully healing her heart as expertly as he had broken it.

She had been so cold and so empty without him. Now

he warmed her, filled her up and brought her to the brink of total gratification but refused to allow her to experience the spine-tingling release only he could give her for long maddening moments. When she thought she would go insane from pleasure, unable to bear it a second longer, he, himself, finally jumped headlong with her into the endless void that led to utter fulfillment.

A long while later, they snuggled together in the bed, content and whole again. He reclined against the headboard and head rested against his chest.

"Does this mean you forgive me?" Nathan asked hopefully.

"Maybe." Marcy smiled, kissed his chest and snuggled closer. "It depends on how good your explanation is, and I guess it's about time you get to it."

She didn't want to talk about the unhappy month they had spent apart, but she knew they had to. She had to know why he had left and assure herself that he wouldn't do it again. However, all she wanted to do was stay curled up next to him, and she couldn't bring herself to move just yet.

"In my defense, I tried to explain before you took advantage of me," he teased, running his fingers through her hair.

She chuckled. "I took advantage of you, huh?"

"Yep." He smiled when she glanced up at him. "And I loved every second of it."

"Me, too," she confessed. Lord, she was glad to have him back. It almost didn't matter why he had left—almost. She rubbed her cheek against his pec before lightly trailing her tongue over the smooth hard muscles of his chest.

"If you don't stop that, though, my explanation's going to be delayed again."

"Okay." She kissed his chest lingeringly, sat up and wrapped a sheet around her. "I'm listening."

"Well, I left because…" His voice trailed off when her fingers began dancing along his chest. "Marcy," he groaned when her fingers earnestly began tracing his six-pack abs.

"I'm sorry." She chuckled, removing her hands and standing up. "There, is that better?"

"Not for me," he quickly denied, adding on a resigned sigh, "But if you want answers, yes."

"I do," she affirmed. "Tell me why you left, Nathan."

He sat up and took her hand and tugged until she was sitting beside him. "I didn't want to. I had to."

"Had to?" She frowned. "Why?"

"I had a mission to carry out." Before she could respond, he continued, "For the past ten years, I've been a part of a covert Black Ops unit. I've been second in command for the last two." He paused, allowing his stunning words to sink in. Her mouth dropped open in shock, and he squeezed her fingers reassuringly. "My team is a rescue unit. I never know where I'm going or how long I'm going to be there. It's the nature of the job."

She blinked rapidly. "Are you kidding me?"

"No," he said and smiled. "I'm deadly serious."

She stared into his eyes for several seconds and realized he was serious. This was the last thing she had expected him to confess. Wow.

"You really are like James Bond," she marveled and he chuckled. "No one knows about this?" At his negative nod, she continued, "Not even your family?"

"No." He tucked her hair behind her ear. "They think I'm a lawyer for the State Department, and I am, but that's my public cover. I've wanted to tell them, but the first oath we take is one of absolute secrecy. In Black Ops, one of our greatest strengths is our anonymity."

"Yes, I suppose it would be," she agreed, stunned.

"Even now, I can't say much about my team, where I've been and what I've done," he apologized. "No one else can know any of this. I'm telling you because I have to." He touched her cheek. "Lord knows you above all people deserve to know why I left the way I did."

"Thank you." She covered his hand with hers. "I won't say anything to anyone," she promised.

"I know you won't." He kissed her gently. "I agonized trying to find the least painful way to leave you when I received my deployment orders, but there was just no good way to do it. I'm sorry, Marcy."

"I believe you." She smiled at him lovingly. "Can you tell me if your mission was a success?"

"It was." He kissed her hands. He had nearly destroyed her, yet she cared enough to ask about a job that had taken him away from her.

"This—the job you do—is why you kept fighting us?"

"Yes, I knew I had to deploy soon, and it wasn't fair to start a relationship with you no matter how much I wanted to."

"But you did, anyway."

"Because—" his fingers played with her hair "—I couldn't resist your charms."

"So, it's my fault." Despite his playful tone, she tensed slightly. "Is that what you're saying?"

"No, Marcy." He stroked her cheek. "I could have stopped all of this before our feelings for each other had a chance to grow out of control."

"How?"

"By making some excuse to my family and leaving New York immediately after the wedding."

"Why didn't you?"

"I should have," he admitted, tracing her lower lip with

his finger. "I knew I was living on borrowed time, but whatever time I had here I wanted to spend with you."

She smiled. "Even though you fought me tooth and nail?"

"I was trying to *make* myself do the right thing by you," he stressed. "You didn't know the secret life I was leading or the dangers therein. I did. I knew better, Marcy, but I couldn't leave you alone, and for that, I'm truly sorry."

"Don't be." She ran her nails across his chin. "I couldn't stay away from you, either."

"When we first met, I felt like I'd been hit by a freight train," he confessed. "I knew immediately you were the one who was more dangerous to me than any adversary I had ever faced in the field."

Her fingers stilled. "You did?"

"Yes." He smiled at her tenderly. "I used to ridicule the other men in my unit when they talked about falling in love, but one look at you and I quickly realized what they had been trying to tell me— When you meet your soul mate, there's absolutely nothing you can do, except give in to fate."

"I'm your soul mate?"

"You are."

"You're mine," she softly admitted before her eyes grew troubled as icy fingers of fear squeezed her heart. "What happens now, Nathan?"

"The job I do is necessary. I know I make a difference." His words intensified her fear. "But—"

"I understand," she interrupted. She did understand, but her heart ached at his admission.

Standing, she walked over to stare out of the window. She heard Nathan get out of bed, and soon he was at her side. He placed a hand on her arm, and she turned to face him.

"What's wrong, baby?"

"Nathan…" She paused before sadly admitting, "I don't know if I can live like this—with you disappearing to parts unknown for weeks or months, not knowing how you are or where. This time almost killed me, and I had no idea you were in danger."

"I know."

"How am I going to live without you?" she whispered brokenly, placing her face in her hands.

"You're not. You didn't let me finish my thought before." He captured her distraught face between his hands, forcing her to meet his eyes. "I'm going to give the job up."

"You can't give up your career for me!" She was thrilled and horrified at his words. "I'd never ask that of you."

"I know you wouldn't," he acknowledged. "I'm not doing it just for you. It's for me and, more importantly, for us." He paused, and she remained silent, not knowing what to say. "Marcy, resentment and anger for the secrecy and lies my job forces me to live with has been brewing in me for some time," he admitted. "The second I met you, I realized just how tired I was of going from place to place not having anywhere to truly call home, not having anyone special to come home to. Being away from you was the most miserable time of my life. The thrill, the danger, the uncertainty of Black Ops used to excite me, but nothing excites me the way you do."

"Nathan…" She shook her head helplessly.

"Marcy, the thought of coming back to you, holding you, simply seeing your smile, hearing your laughter was what got me through the past miserable month. I want you. I want a life with you more than I want anything else in this world."

"Are you absolutely sure?" Hope sprang to life within her.

"Yes, I was debriefed a week ago, and then I quit. It was

the only way I could allow myself to return to you to offer you the life you deserve." His fingers ran through her hair, and her hands rested on his wrists.

"Was it that easy to quit?"

"They didn't want to let me go," he slowly admitted. "But after they heard my lack of concentration almost jeopardized my last mission and I assured them it would happen again and again if they didn't accept my resignation, they agreed with me. They know it's to their advantage to have a happy ex-soldier than a disgruntled, distracted and dangerous active one."

"They won't call you again someday out of the blue?" She voiced her worst fear.

"No, I've more than done my time protecting my country. Now it's time to concentrate on building a life—with you. I won't ever leave you again, Marcy," he promised, taking her hands in his.

"Nathan, I was so sad when you left." She allowed all the pain she had so carefully kept at bay to break free. "You broke my heart."

"I know, baby, and I'm so sorry." He pulled her into his arms. "I won't ever do it again. I promise."

"Promise?" she whispered against his shoulder.

"Yes, on my life," he vowed, kissing her hair.

"Then, I'll follow you anywhere as long as we can be together," she vowed, pulling back to stare at him.

"You'd leave New York for me?"

"Just give me time to pack," she laughingly amended. "In fact, forget packing."

"I love you, Marcy." He kissed her lingeringly.

"I love you, too," she whispered, arms circling his neck.

"I would never ask you to leave your home, your family or your career," he firmly stated.

"I don't mind." He had made a great sacrifice for her; she wanted him to know she would make one for him.

"I know, but I do." His lips nipped at hers. "I'm leaving Washington and coming back to New York."

"Are you sure?" She couldn't believe how wonderfully everything was working itself out.

"Yes, very." He nodded. "Washington was never a home, only a place I worked and slept. My home is with you, Marcy."

He released her to bend down and pick up his jacket from the floor. Taking a black velvet box out of the pocket, he opened it revealing a gorgeous pear-shaped diamond surrounded by emeralds.

"Nathan…" She placed a hand to her mouth in shock.

"Marcy—" he took her hand in his "—I love you so much. Be my wife. Be the mother of my children. You're already my life."

"You take initiative very well once you get warmed up." She spoke through tears, eyes lifting from the ring to lock on his.

"Is that a yes?"

He took the ring from its bed. She fought back a sob of happiness as he placed it on her finger. It fit perfectly— just like them.

"That's an unequivocal yes." She pressed her lips to his. "I can't wait to tell everybody."

"Want to tell them now?" His eyebrow lifted as his hands ran down her bare shoulders and back.

"Later," she whispered against his mouth and then pulled back and chuckled. "I'd better tell Dami over the phone. He'll probably strangle you first and ask questions later if we just show up."

"You sound like you'd rather enjoy seeing that," he accused around a smile.

"How can you accuse me of such a thing?" She chuckled, pressing closer. "Although I did devise some ingenious ways to torture you myself."

"Is that right?"

"Mmm-hmm." She ran her hands down his powerful arms. "You have a lot of making up to do, mister."

"Gladly." He kissed her hard. "We'll call everyone much later," he whispered against her neck as his hands deftly pulled the sheet from her to pool at her feet, hands running over her.

"Later like tomorrow," she agreed, sighing as his mouth slid from one shoulder, across her collarbone to the other.

"Late tomorrow—or the next day," he groaned and she laughed, sliding her fingers across his shoulders down his back.

"Mmm, that sounds like a plan," she agreed. "I—"

Her words were effectively and pleasantly silenced by his hot, hungry mouth and then further words were forgotten.

Two days later, Nathan and Marcy saw their families and told them they were engaged. To be expected, no one understood the need for Nathan's hasty departure, though everyone knew why he had come back. They were simply glad that he and Marcy were together again for good this time—everyone except Damien.

"You promised you wouldn't hurt her?" Damien tightly reminded once he and Nathan were alone.

"I know." Nathan nodded. "It was unavoidable."

"What about the next time?" Damien's eyes held a warning.

"There won't be a next time, not like this," Nathan promised.

"Forgive me if I don't believe you."

"Damien, I understand your anger toward me, and it's justified. I wish I could explain why I did what I did to everyone's satisfaction, but I can't." He paused. "I've explained my actions to the one person who really matters—Marcy. She understands and has forgiven me and agreed to be my wife. That should be all that matters," Nathan ended.

They stared at each other in challenge—neither saying anything for several minutes. Damien folded his arms over his chest and then smiled—ever so slightly.

"You're right." Damien slowly extended his hand toward the other man.

He still wanted to beat him to a pulp for hurting his sister, but for Marcy's sake, he resisted. He had watched them all evening, and they were obviously very happy and very much in love. Whatever Nathan's reasons for leaving, Marcy understood and had decided to forgive him. She wanted to spend her life with him. As much as he loved and wanted to protect her, it wasn't his place to question or try to ruin her happiness but rather to understand and trust that she knew what she was doing.

"I'll make her happy," Nathan promised as he shook Damien's hand.

"You already do." Damien's smile broadened as he glanced at his sister who stood across the room between his wife and her sister staring anxiously at them.

"Whew!" Marcy let out her breath loudly. "I thought they were going to come to blows."

"So did I." Natasha similarly released her breath.

"They seem to have settled things," Nicole observed as the men in question who were now somewhat relaxed with each other instead of on edge as they had been a few seconds earlier.

"Thank goodness!" Marcy beamed, hugging both women. "I'm so happy!"

"You deserve to be," Nicole replied and Natasha seconded.

"Nicole, you're not jeopardizing your job by staying a week late for the wedding, are you?" Marcy voiced concern.

"No. Everything will be fine," Nicole assured.

She silently prayed she was speaking the truth. Alexander James had not seemed at all happy when she had phoned him about the delay. In fact, she had half expected him to tell her not to bother coming to Paris at all. Well, she wouldn't worry about that now. The most important thing was to be home for Marcy and her brother's wedding, and if Alexander James didn't like it, tough!

"Do you have enough time to make the gowns?" Natasha interrupted her thoughts.

"I'll work night and day if necessary," Nicole promised.

"I love you both, my two sisters." Marcy had joy overflowing from her heart. It should be illegal to be so happy.

"We love you, too," Natasha and Nicole echoed as they both kissed each of her cheeks.

"Well, Linda, despite a few tense moments, we made a good match, didn't we?" Margaret smiled as they watched Marcy float over to Nathan, who smiled lovingly at her as she snuggled into his arms.

"Perfect," Linda agreed. "Luckily, Nathan didn't spoil things with his peculiar disappearing act." She sighed heavily as she remembered the weeks of agony that had caused everyone concerned.

"That's all over with now. All that matters is that he and Marcy are together and happy and they're going to stay that way," Margaret firmly predicted.

"I wish he would tell us why he left." Michael frowned.

"It doesn't matter." Margaret smiled at him, and he nodded in agreement following her eyes as they rested on their daughter's deliriously happy face—nothing mattered except the joy their baby exuded because of the man in whose arms she now resided.

"You're right," Lincoln agreed. "True love triumphs all."

"Well said," Michael replied, and their wives smiled in agreement.

"It's too bad you don't have another son for Nicole." Linda's brow furrowed in contemplation. "I think it's time she thought about settling down."

"Well, I'm sure if we put our heads together, we can find a suitable young man for her." Margaret was thrilled about the new challenge.

"I'm sure you're right." Linda smiled in agreement. "What about, what was his name? Henry?"

"Hmm." Margaret's brow furrowed contemplatively. "Henry? Yes. Could be," Margaret agreed as they walked off arm in arm.

"What are we going to do with them?" Michael asked Lincoln, who shrugged and shook his head.

"In thirty-nine years, I haven't been able to find a solution to Linda's meddling. If you come up with a plan, let me know." Lincoln slapped his friend on the back as they walked over to the bar to get another drink.

"Women and matchmaking go together like franks and beans." Michael sighed as he picked up a glass of whiskey and raised it in a toast.

"I'll drink to that." Lincoln clinked his glass with his own, and they downed the contents before laughing loudly.

"Well," Nathan said as his arms encircled Marcy's waist, "all things considered, I think this impromptu family meeting is going quite well."

"I wouldn't stand for anything less." Marcy laughed, but sobered quickly and asked, "Are you and Damien okay?"

"We're fine."

"Good," she approved. "I'm so happy, Nathan."

"And I plan to keep you that way."

"Just love me, never leave me again and you will."

"That, I can easily do." He kissed her lingeringly. "I love our family, but I can't wait to get you alone."

"Mmm." Marcy pressed closer. "What do you have in mind?"

"I'll show you when we get home," he promised with a wolfish grin.

"Give me a little preview," she softly ordered.

"Gladly," he agreed, capturing her lips again in a thorough, spine-tingling kiss.

Epilogue

Marcy and Nathan were married a week later in as private a ceremony as their mothers would allow. Marcy was a beautiful bride dressed in a figure-hugging satin gown of pristine white. The sweetheart neckline and bodice were covered in lace as were her quarter sleeves and slight train billowing behind her as she had walked down the aisle toward the man of her dreams. Her hair had been pulled back from her face, cascading down her back in layered curls. Nicole had been her maid of honor, and Natasha had been one of her bridesmaids.

Marcy flowed into Nathan's arms as they slowly moved around the empty dance floor while their loved ones and friends looked on.

"Happy?" Nathan asked as they barely moved.

"Deliriously."

"You're so beautiful." His eyes exuded love.

"Thank you," she whispered. "And you're very handsome—and sweet." She couldn't resist adding the latter.

"Marcy, I've told you I am not sweet," he responded in exasperation as she knew he would.

"Oh, yes, you are," she argued, fingers playing with his chin. "And I'm going to keep reminded you of that fact," she promised and laughed as he pretended to be annoyed.

"I don't know why I love you so," he lightly remarked.

"Because I'm irresistible," she quickly shot back.

"Very sure of yourself, aren't you?" The hand on her waist pulled her closer.

"As certain as I always was that we would end up right here," she confidently informed him, outlining his lower lip with her fingernail causing his eyes to darken noticeably.

"You were right." His arm tightened around her.

"I usually am," she said and chuckled. "You should remember that."

"Yes, Mrs. Carter," he said and returned her smile.

"I love the sound of that."

"So do I. We belong together."

"We do, and you've known that all along." She smiled. "But being a man, you had to try and fight the inevitable."

"Being a woman, you wouldn't allow me to succeed," he teased.

"Sometimes it does pay to be relentless." She laughed as they suddenly came to a halt in the middle of the dance floor.

"In dividends," he agreed, lowering his mouth to hers.

"I love you, Nathan," she whispered as her arms encircled his neck.

"I love you back—always," he echoed. "I can't wait to start our honeymoon."

"Why wait?" Marcy impishly smiled. "Let's start right now."

Nathan groaned. "I love the way you think."

Regardless of their audience, their lips drifted together in a heated kiss echoing a promise of undying love.

* * * * *

Hot summertime reading....

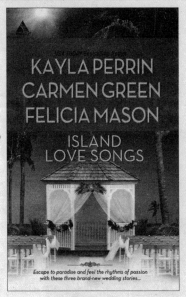

KAYLA PERRIN
CARMEN GREEN
FELICIA MASON

ISLAND LOVE SONGS

Escape to paradise and feel the rhythms of passion
with these three brand-new wedding stories...

ISLAND LOVE SONGS

USA TODAY
Bestselling Author
KAYLA PERRIN

CARMEN GREEN

FELICIA MASON

Talented writers bring you three romantic stories about weddings in paradise! Enjoy the adventures of three couples as they create sizzling memories in exotic locales!

HARLEQUIN®
www.Harlequin.com

*Available August 2013
wherever books are sold!*

KPILS1370813

The perfect stories to indulge in...

Hollington Homecoming

VOLUME ONE

SANDRA KITT
ESSENCE BESTSELLING AUTHOR
JACQUELIN THOMAS

Experience the drama and passion as eight friends reunite in Atlanta for their ten-year college reunion! This collection features the first two full-length novels in the Hollington Homecoming series, *RSVP with Love* by Sandra Kitt and *Teach Me Tonight* by Jacquelin Thomas.

"This heartwarming story has characters that grow and mature beautifully."
—RT Book Reviews on RSVP WITH LOVE

Available August 2013 wherever books are sold!

And coming in September, HOLLINGTON HOMECOMING VOLUME TWO, featuring Pamela Yaye and Adrianne Byrd

HARLEQUIN®
www.Harlequin.com

REQUEST YOUR FREE BOOKS!

2 FREE NOVELS
PLUS 2 *FREE GIFTS!*

KIMANI™ ROMANCE

Love's ultimate destination!

*The conclusion to the
Hideaway Wedding
trilogy!*

**National Bestselling
Author**

**ROCHELLE
ALERS**

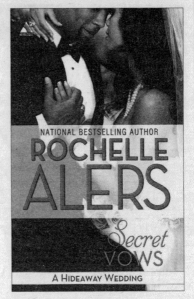

Twins Ana and Jason and their cousin Nicholas are successful
thirtysomethings who are single—and loving it. They have no idea that
their relatives are betting on which one of them will get married first! But
by the family's New Year's Eve reunion, will all three have learned what it
means to be really lucky—in love?

Music is Jason Cole's first love and so far, no woman has ever come close.
Until the gorgeous new waitress at the local restaurant catches his eye…
and his heart! But Greer Evans has a secret, putting everything they share
on the line….

**"Smoking-hot love scenes, a fascinating story and extremely
likable characters combine in a thrilling book that's hard to put
down." —*RT Book Reviews* on *Sweet Dreams***

www.Harlequin.com

*Available July 2013
wherever books are sold!*